Alistair Fruish

KISS MY ASBO

First Publication
LEPUS BOOKS
2013

ISBN: 978-0-9572535-2-0

LEPUS BOOKS

www.lepusbooks.co.uk

For James Linell

Many thanks to John Row, Geraldine Ryan, Jamie Delano, Quentin Seddon, Barry Hale, Lindsay Spence and Alan Moore.

PART ONE

Double Bubble

My Dad spiked me with a powerful mind-altering drug. He loved me and thought that it would make up for never helping with my homework. The homework he always insisted that I did. I didn't get much help from Mum, she lives out of town and it gets tricky when we see each other.

Maybe I could turn this into a comic. Start with a panel the size of a whole page. Uncle Vic hands over the electric blue smartie to Dad. It would be good if Vic were in a black military uniform with yellow rank markings. Dad all belly in his cheesy Hawaiian shirt, standing in the dark middle of The Firs. They're the woods on the other side of what's left of the Heath, in the direction of the planted Princess. I see sharp beams of sunlight like death-rays penetrating the dark pillars of pine around them. The pill in Vic's hand's a super glow-worm. It shines up on their faces and down on the millions of wood ants swarming at their feet. These ants march in step to spell out a title, which will be: The Straight Dope.

The panel would contain two balloons; one for speech and one for thought. The dialogue in the speech bubble is from Dad, saying, "Any side effects?" The thought bubble that hovers over Vic's head contains five other thought bubbles, which also contain thought bubbles, and so on. And in each thought balloon would be a unique mark, like a hieroglyph.

It's very likely that it didn't happen that way. (It would be a good way to start the comic though.) Dad was probably cotched in front of the TV drinking brew and burning weed. Vic wasn't around very long and I didn't see him. He never hung in these ends too long. Don't blame him. My main memory of him is of a tall man, sullen looking. Muscle upon muscle. He didn't pay attention to us kids at family dos and stuff. Dad said that what Vic did was secret, that I should maybe think about joining the army too. Perhaps he was trying to offer me a way out of the Estate, show it could be done without flitting off with a junkie to Welwyn Garden City, like Mum. He used to say that Vic was the only good example in our family, even though I knew he hated him. He dissed him to everyone else, except Gran. It was a bit of a mixed message. Dad's good at those. I always thought that the so-called secret job probably meant Vic did something boring and was pretending to be more interesting than he was really up to. Seems I was wrong there. I was wrong about a lot of things back before Dad spiked me.

It was juss a few weeks after the Olympics had finished in London; a couple of weeks after Vic had chipped from the Estate, and the day before I went back to school, when a couple of military police turned up looking for him. I wasn't going to let them talk to me. I had a suspicion that it was about the smartie, and if they talked to me, they might figure something out. I thought of Dad's mantra: "Don't bring no beast t' the yard!" Uncle Vic had gone and done it now. Dad nearly crapped himself trying to hide the weed before he let them in, but they weren't bothered about a seedy old toker. They were very cagey about what they wanted Vic for. Tried to scare Dad by saying failure to tell them anything would be considered treason and that you can still be hung for that. Little did they know that talking to beast, even military beast, was a bigger treason to my old man. He wasn't going to grass even if he hated his brother, though I wasn't so sure he did anymore. He acted like a dumb old stoner. Told them nothing. Why exactly his feelings had changed toward his brother I wasn't sure until later. He really seemed proud when he spoke about him. I stayed out of the way. I left my mobile on audio record in the living room, then took off out the back and got a bus into town.

Northampton is about as far in England as you can get from the sea – should be OK here when the ice caps melt, innit? Can't think of any other reason to live here. It's the biggest town in Europe, but it only takes a quarter of an hour on a bus to get from the edge into the centre. The bus station exists to sap the remaining will of the people who use it. It resembles the docking bay of the Death Star as you're mercilessly pulled into it on a tractor beam of boredom. Except I'd never felt so unbored. Strange intuitions, feelings about things that were not obviously connected, seemed to come to me. The air under pressure in the wheels of the bus, I thought about that for ages. I was struck by the beauty of valves, and figured out how to increase the power of an air-pistol I'd found in the attic at Gran's the summer before. I thought about the wind and thought about the precious bubble of atmosphere that normally goes unnoticed as we swim in it. Like my own mind had been to me in the past. Air and mind, both invisible in a sense. We notice them more when they change. As soon as I got into town I got straight back on a bus and went home.

I was gone for about an hour. When I got back the cops had gone. I have the whole of Dad's interrogation stored as a wav file: the best bit is at the beginning with Dad running around freaking out. I should post it on the net one day.

Before I swallowed the blue smartie, hidden out in the open, stuck on top of some Cornish ice cream that Dad gave me, I was certain about a lot of things. Now I am no longer certain. There seems to be a lot more in the way of possibilities and maybes. Yet in another way it all seems simple. Everything I feel or think about seems different now. Like there are these alternatives I wouldn't have grasped before. I feel like they were probably always there, but I was closed off to them. Like when a fridge turns off, you become aware that it was humming all along, but you only notice it when it's gone. It's like these possibilities flicker in and out of existence in a way that makes me notice them. Words – they're so interesting. Ra! How could I have not noticed that before? Somehow the smartie has changed me but left me the same. Well, to look at.

Earl and Darren started to notice once I got back to school. In a sense I suppose they became my victims, or maybe I was their saviour. I was still getting on with them like before, but Darren was starting to annoy me. When I asked him to lend me a tenner, he said only for double bubble. That pissed me off. A tenner to borrow a tenner! Tosser. This joker was supposed to be my spar, my bredren. I suppose that this planted some of the seeds of what was to follow.

Vic told my Dad that it would be permanent for him; but I'm a lot younger, so who knows? I didn't realise anything was different to start off with. The drug zonked me. I slept for about a week. Thought I'd juss got the lurgie. I think Dad was really worried that my brain might rot and I would be permanently crystallised in the quilt: comatose, sparko, a chrysalis of cotton and fever sweat. I'm glad he was worried. Serves him right. Dad's never been too hot at the forward thinking. Probably juss as well he didn't call a doctor in. Still, what's done is done. Sometimes you can make the right choice for the wrong reasons. I have faint memories of him telling me stories as I recovered.

He muss have made them up: he's not too hot at reading. It made me remember a time when he was away and he sent me a CD of tales he made up. There was one about a monster called a Grisilore. It would always want twice as much back as it gave out and kept the whole Kingdom poor. I guess that type of behaviour upset Dad too. I used to listen to that CD every night at Gran's. I still have it somewhere.

All that wire and the dogs, it was kind of like school. I used to hate visiting him in that place, except on the days when he was freed. I'd bunk off to meet him at the gates, if I could get a bus out there. Help him carry his stuff in a bin liner. Then we'd hang out together for the whole day.

If I was going to tell this for Hollywood it'd be about the military accidentally developing pills that made you super attractive and irresistible. No one is interested in smarts. It's all about being famous or getting respec'.

I can't think of anyone who's famous for having ideas that wasn't some kind of businessman or politician. They seem like hypnotists to me now. It's clear that the cleverest people are not in charge, or at least they're not on TV much: but where are they? I need to read more. Perhaps I can find out. Now I can read a book in about half an hour and remember it all. I read more books yesterday than I read last year.

It wasn't until I'd eaten Uncle Vic's blue pill that I started to realise how angry I had been with Dad. Mum as well. I knew I was angry with her; but I didn't know why. I'm working on that. It had a lot to do with Mum, what I did, I guess. If she hates me the whole world might as well hate me. Realising I was angry with Dad was more of a surprise to me. It's not as if Vic's pill was a miracle that suddenly cured everything. I'd hidden a lot of it from myself. Took it out on others. Probably on Mum's boyfriend the most, though he is a muppet. Various teachers and adults in general made me miserable so I'd piss them off by withdrawing. I muss have taken a lot in during school, but I didn't think I remembered much of it. Not until I woke up. Now I seem to have this fantastic memory bank full of all sorts of information that I can cross connect and get lost in. It's like someone has opened the curtains and light has flooded in, making my dusty brain zing. So I've made a few mistakes. Juss because I've taken a drug that's made me smart doesn't mean I don't still make mistakes. It's juss that I tend to look at problems as something to face, more than I did before.

The government have supposedly banned smart drugs in schools until their long-term safety is known. This isn't stopping the rich kids taking them. If you know who's juggling them you can get them, but they're pricey. I don't know anyone who has ever taken any. The politicians are probably chucking them down so they can figure out how to screw everybody even more. It's mostly juss weed in my school though. No one is rich. Most of my crew want to be, and famous. When Dad was at school it was all sniffing glue. Back in the day he was the only one blazing, so he says. According to him, "It's an improvement, the herb is sacred." I guess that's how he justifies supplying Earl. He gets uppity about the stronger shit, like crack and what-not. That's probably got a lot to do with Mum. He wouldn't like it if he knew that Darren was dabbling, but he wouldn't be surprised - this is the Estate after all. One thing I seem to have lost interest in is weed. I suppose I never had much really; that's Dad's thing. The plant is interesting though, and beautiful. Maybe I'll grow it one day.

I guess in his own daft way Dad juss wanted to give me the same chances that the rich kids get. It seems that Uncle Vic's blue pill was some kind of military dope. An ultra-smart drug. One hit, and if you survive, you're massively more intelligent. I feel a bit vain putting it like that, but it seems that's what's happened. It's not that I was thick before; it's juss that I have so many more choices now. But that's OK. Despite what's happened, I think everything is going to get better.

I first realised something was different when I went back to school, after being virtually unconscious for a week. Actually, as soon as I really woke up I knew something was different. But other people can be our mirrors sometimes, and they helped me to see it more clearly. I was in the bogs, hanging with Darren and Earl, talking about the Olympics that had been happening over the summer, discussing whether or not skateboarding was an Olympic sport and if they had an equivalent in ancient Greece. The school had got the drug dogs in again, and I spotted them out of the window. Darren and Earl wanted to flush the shit they got from Dad, but I wouldn't let them. In the past Earl would've made the decisions. But in the space of two minutes I thought of hundreds of plans. Finally I got Darren to get out his blade. Then I got Earl to take out the in-soles from his trainers. I sliced through them width-wise like cutting up a roll. I ran Darren's lighter flame gently over them for a few minutes then got an old condom out of my keyring holder that I kept as a kind of charm to bring good luck in the shag department (it hadn't worked). I rubbed the in-soles all over my body then my friends did the same, as they laughed and cussed me for cheesing up their threads. Then I wrapped up the weed in the Odour Eaters, pulled the condom over the parcel and tied up the end tight, folding the plastic back over on itself. Then I stuck it under the tap with loads of soap, washed everything, dried off the parcel, put my hands under the hand-blower and stuck the packet in my pocket. Earl and Darren thought I'd gone mental. I should juss cork it, or flush it. I'd never behaved like this before. They didn't know what to do. I told them to chill and wash their hands and faces, I'd take the fall if anything went down. I walked out onto the corridor, straight into the path of the dog, and nothing happened.

Uncle Vic had taken it himself as part of a government experiment. Top secret, that's what he told Dad. One of the effects of the drug was to make him realise that he should sort out his differences with Dad. So he stole some of the blue pills and the details of how to make them. Then he rocked up in Northampton and told Dad that he was going into the drug business, the army was no longer relevant. They could go to Hell, all war was pointless, and the ones we were fighting especially so. The only war worth fighting was the war against wars. His bosses were sitting on this stuff and he was going to let it out. The risk was worth taking. The entire world should have these smarties. He was going abroad. Expect some kind of message. He'd juss walked out – went AWOL. I thought he sounded like a crusty, or a hedge monkey, and perhaps he'd gone a bit nuts. But Dad said it was something else. Something he'd never seen in him before. Sanity.

Vic told Dad that he was sorry for all that had gone down with them. That he loved him, and that he had something special for him: that he muss take it and be prepared to stay in bed for a week. Dad was flabbergasted. But I guess I can see why the bastard gave it to me. It had radically transformed his meathead brother – what would it do to him? So being the small time drug-dealing scumbag that he is, he tested it out on me. The one that he hoped would not grow up to be like him, even though he enjoyed being him. He probably made the right choice. Still fair's fair. If I get the chance and get hold of some more of those smarties, I would spike him right back.

The day before we did it we went for a walk after school and ended up out on the meadow. Earl and Darren were watching a stolen moped burn down by the railway line and talking the usual crap. I asked Darren what would be the best way to create more chances in our area and he said, "Move the red light district up here, innit?" There was some truth in that.

Black smoke from the burning bike drifted over the rails and across the fields towards the Firs. I wanted to carry on walking, but Earl was coming on all tough, rapping about how this was all Earl's land, and that we should call him 'The Earl', and that we could go no further unless he allowed us to go on. It was indeed all the Earl's land, but a different Earl.

I think Earl was finding the changes in my brain difficult to deal with. I was now a threat to his idea of himself as the boss and he was starting to throw his weight around a bit. I dared Earl in front of Darren knowing he'd have to say yes. I don't know where it came from. He was bigging himself up as usual. It never used to bother me, but now it was starting to get on my nerves. I didn't think. I juss said it: "What's the point in school? Let's face it, we're either going to end up unemployed, in prison, or working in the bake house like everybody else. Let's do something pucker, that'll get us proper respect. You wanna be famous, right?" They agreed. So I continued, "Let's juss walk a couple of miles over there and dig up the body of the Princess. Then we'll be famous and can ketch props and maybe make a raise." I knew I was forcing Earl's hand when I said, "I'll do it myself if you're not up to it."

The main problem for Darren was there was no obvious money in it. He thought we should ransom her skull. I told him he was more likely to get his tunes played if we said it was a protest. I could see he was hesitating. Then I thought of what would swing him, "Bring your mobile and take some pictures.

You can sell those on the internet." He bought that.

"Ok," he said, "let's do it." He was in.

Uncle Vic's pill was connected to what I did. I would never have thought of it before. I certainly understand myself more and more since I took it. But you don't understand yourself completely overnight, even with hardcore military aid. Darren and Earl hadn't really thought about the consequences – they were too busy thinking about how to load the footage up onto the net. But I knew what I was doing. I didn't know why. Now that I've had some time to think about it a lot, I feel I know some of the reasons. I was making myself pay twice. Bursting the bubble of my world again.

Bringing the buried past into the present. I think that's what a lot of crimes are – ways of repeating a pattern. Hurting yourself some more.

The next evening I cleaned the weed from Dad's. Later I put it in his old hiding place in the woods as we walked through them on our mission with destiny. Dad would go mad when he got in, but he'd be glad if the beast kicked his door in later on. I got a spade, Darren's brother's inflatable dingy, and a torch. Then we checked out the location on Google Earth. We walked there easily enough, climbed the wall and headed for the lake.

PART TWO

Kiss My ASBO

There is a cure for being intelligent. It goes by the name of love. It works for most people. Not juss those who have been micky-finned with thought boosting meds by their own Pa. My capacity for wot'liss behaviour increased rapidly as the antidote kicked in.

Strange and attractive, that's what she was. Right at the outset I was susceptible to her ways. Conditions at the beginning mark all of us: triggers, back in the nitty-gritty at the start, propel us into aggravating up-shots. From the get-go, minted or in a ghetto, forces beyond our control brand us; shape our lives; limit us: sell us out at a cut throat price, for real. Common patterns crop up, but no two entrance wounds are the same: you might recover from the birth blast in a way that wasn't guessed, or stay sawn off at the knees, your whole life an unoriginal nosedive. Impact, it's a hard thing to gauge. So, you never know exactly how stuff's going to go down. It was the way she got me to make her a cup of coffee before the interview that started it. Her chaotic hair dyed bright green. Little stuff makes the difference, to it all. She gave me her full attention. I should have thought more about why.

You can see how it makes sense that when we are linked-up deep; we fail to see the flaws. Sticking together can be useful. You need to choose wisely those you care about. I suppose people don't have much choice when it comes to their family. Perhaps it was a sign of brains on Mum's part that she took off. Certainly I started to lose mine when I met Samantha Mir. Though there are some people who would have beef with me about that, on the grounds that I met her after setting off to dig up the body of a Princess - which wasn't generally considered to be a very clever idea. Certainly that was Dad's point of view, when he spilled one. I think he was starting to regret giving me the pill. The first question he asked when he saw me again was, "Weh it deh?" meaning his ganja, that I had stashed in the woods. Dad was lost without the good-good. I had stolen his girlfriend then hidden her body in the pines. Faithful always to Mary Jane his one true love dat his eedjat picney 'ad teefed from him. Sweet Green he called her sometimes, but regular it was juss, "draw". No bush weed or hybrid punk for him. Due reverence muss be given to the sacrament of lambsbread. His own personal stash which he wanted back: now. His love for this illegal female could be a problem given we were in a court. He had to keep his voice low else I think he might have even shouted at me. He rarely did that. In all my life he never hit me, ever. Even though his own Dad had clouted 'n' clapped him all the time, apparently. As I was growing up, one of the tings he would say was, "Granfada Livingston living still bwoy, you'd kech beats." For all the shit you could say about my Dad, he was still my Dad. He cared for me the best he could, though regular he hackled me hard, vexed me proper furious sometimes. Still he had one big ting going for him, which made up for all he'd done in the past: he'd stepped up. He might not have been the brightest candle jammed in the mini-Bakewell, but maybe that allowed him to put up with me. Once he found out what I had done, all he said about it then was that she was not even buried there.

"Man dat island ting is a fake, trus me."

He told me that his people who had reached to those sides around those times, had seen stuff that made them think she was in the village church with the rest of her mob. Then he made me laugh by telling me he once had a plan to switch signs on the roads: re-direct tourists on to one of the bad endz. Seeing as how the two very different kinds of estate had the same name and were juss a few miles apart, it wouldn't be so hard.

Samantha, at least understood. She understood far too much at the start, in the end maybe not enough. I had regular appointments with her that began straight after the hearing. I didn't think that was unusual at the time. I had juss tried to dig up the body of a Princess. I had never been in a court before. Mum and Dad always kept me out of their fuckry. ASBOs and reporting restrictions were all new to me. An ASBO: me nuh bizniz. It would at least give me props out on road.

When you think back to events in your past why is it that your thoughts never seem to play in rewind, recalling it all backwards like on a DVD? It always starts further away in time then steps forwards. Even though it has been chemically enhanced my memory is not like video, but now it does seem to have a stunning freeze frame. I have this jam-packed recall. Sometimes it's so vivid I can get the impression I am still there in the past, doing whatever I was doing then. What has happened has yet to happen, I can do things differently this time. But it's an illusion, there's no going back to change. If I try to make the scenes play out differently, the experience morphs. There seems to have been a revolution in the info that springs into my mind. I have more of an inkling of what I am actually remembering opposed to what I might be making up. My feelings transform the recordings. I never realised before how creative memory is. It is always filling in the blanks. These days I have some insight into what I am actually recalling, compared to what I am manufacturing.

Difficult for me to be sure I suppose but that's life, for real. It's like the difference between a fading sepia snap and a projected 3D colour film at the cinema, but it is not juss visual. All memories from before I took the pill are faint compared with the impact that life has on my bonce since Dad spiked the ice cream.

Feels like an improvement to me. Most of the time I am less of a moody handle-flying tosser, more aware of what I need to let go. I see possibilities where before I would have lost it, or sulked. That's most of the time. The problem is now when I blow, I blow deep and cold - I put all of my new found brainpower into making an impression.

It's very clear in my mind the first time I told Samantha of how it had gone down as she sat sipping coffee in that room in the Court building. She listened intently. I was relaxed. On the wall behind her there was a picture of trees, the same shade as the blue of her eyes; so similar to Mum's. I described to her the bonelike branches that we walked under as we headed towards the lake. I saw the lights of the house like a movie set in the distance. I told her how I had felt the hand of history on my shoulder. Unfortunately it was delivering a Vulcan nerve pinch. We walked straight into heat.

Thwarted in our desire to achieve pure simple fame that would last beyond our lifetimes. Disinterring the body should have been one of the crimes of the century - but we were out flanked. Juss before we were captured I reminded Darren that we were all to say that this was a protest.

"Yeah right. Against wha'?" he snorted.

"Tings," I told him.

He juss laughed. As we walked towards the lake, after climbing the estate wall, he began re-branding us all. The latest remixed vision for airwave ascendancy transformed us all into *The Piratical Diggers*. Juss *Diggers* would have been slicker, or *Skull-Duggerous Diggers*, maybe. I didn't bother arguing. Earl and me were press-ganged into service as his backing band of buccaneers, carrying our inflatable boat towards an unknown audio shore. He was always thinking up personas for his non-existent career, musical smoke screens to hide behind. That was his lick. Turn everything into a sound-clash; then make man pay-in-full to get in. If Darren's running the dancehall, manz will probably have to pay to get out too. Tonight's headline performance, on the world stage, was to be: *Piratical Privateers vs. Privates of the Private Army*. There were to be no headlines however.

The security guards won that particular battle for the mic. Watchies wuz chooned; tactics dem raw; a sound system in place. Darren didn't enjoy his sample of the violence: popped him right in the face. Dat t'umping rhythm not unexpected: discordant - painful, yet tediously familiar. Generic though they were, McSecurity were more effective in their delivery of repetitive beats than us. Blue bwoy dem wuz heavy,

22

selecta bassline moves, low and sneaky, that left no ska. The cash-cops had mastered the ceremony of urban-jungle combat. They would toast to an easy vank. As they took us to the bridge, Earl went mento. Buss my trance. He spun dem - shook it loose, a lucky break, beat away dem, landed three consecutive hits - dub, dub, dub: stepped up deh pressure, turned tables. Mixed it up a bit. Managed t' step, hotstepp: rewind. Deck one, solo, jam'im, freestyle: bash men, mash up dem, kick in da roots, pitch man inna grime - scratch some respec'. Righteous. They got pretty hardcore after that: spitting acid, rapping knuckles, swinging clubs and drumming heads. Broken: our show was over before it began. My heart went gabba, I gasped for breath. They restrained us, then marched us off to their windowless van - improvised a few bars. Later they would make us sing.

We didn't even get to the lake.

"Mussa triggered some kind of alarm system," I said to Darren who told me his mobile got buss in the commotion so he failed to film anything. A feisty likkle wretch had bruk his tings. Zero shots for the hero shotta. He turned all screwface, vexed because there would be nothing to sell. No recordings equalled neesh *p*. A knock-back on the potential proceeds, all those pounds, profits and pay-checks, they slipped away to nada - powder in the wind. Poor D, his grand gold goals had gone westerly: plans blown - never grasp those Gs now. My man moped for a while, sulking in silence. Dreams all mash up. I tried to talk to him, but he told me to jog-on. I felt noway. Darren often got didgi. He was probably in withdrawal from nicotine. Rude bwoy craven for smokes. The goons had taxed his burn when they'd padded us down.

Earl on the other hand seemed quite jolly. He liked a scrap, with fists or weapons. He was quite capable of stabbing up a man, or so he always said. I'd taken a few precautions. I de-shanked them both before we left Dad's, juss in case it got messy. It wasn't a night to dead a man. I never liked blades. Earl fucked up my shin playing splits with a machete back in ancient history; I went off shivs after that. Earl gave it all the spiel about being a bad-minded yoot wid a cutlass, but I think he was juss an excitement freak deep down beneath the gobshite. Always mucking about, his developing taste for power grew rapidly up from a soil of wild hormones. Anything that got the adrenaline pumping would have been criss as far as he was concerned. He was always like that. Used to jump off of stuff a lot when we were kids: moving car-bonnets, out of trees, you get me? Thought he was Spiderman. Earl would pester him so relentless that his brother would peg our crew as far as the woods, cussin' us off as we tried to leg away. He promised us delicious violence if he caught us. "Eediat bwoy, nuff man dead for less."

Hell awaited the scallywags that teefed his tings, all-fruits-ripe when the day come him personally descend us down to blood fy-yah. Once we were waiting as Earl led him into range. He was burning after his brother on a stolen moped across the heath, when we shot him up the arse with an air rifle. That was sweet.

There is a bond between things that are wrong, and things that are funny.

When the Tescops had got through the palaver of capturing us they began the rigmarole of interrogating us: the three pillocks, who were in their opinion a confounded nuisance. In loud voices they told us that this was private property, asked us why hadn't we stopped when commanded; why had we assaulted them; what the fuck were we doing there; and who the fuck were we? So we told them. Ordinarily we would have stayed shtumm, but that did not fit with our program for international infamy and bare bad-man-ness. We were repping the Estate. The Endz justified the means. Beans got spilt. What form would the beanstalk take? In a way it would turn out to be Samantha.

One of the securities, the older one, seemed to be in charge of the group that captured us. He was local, had an accent juss like Darren's Dad. Darren had a touch of it too. When he said, "you're from round here?" it sounded like, "frum reindeer".

We told him we were local lads.

"Frum tain?" he said, "Nuthampton? Bornunbred?"

Muss have been like how everyone used to talk like "reindeer" time ago when they started building the estates.

"Yiss lad, speck yore gooing tuhbe knee deep in it, entcha?"

I think he too sensed that his moment had come. He might make an interview on the news maybe even a reward, possibly a medal. His chances of jooking his wife juss increased. But he was wrong, nobody would ever hear about it. He pushed us into the van. He locked the door. His hand banged the side of the truck. He shouted, "Thinkont miscreants." He paused. Then added, "Yorl atter frez. Arm buggud if io'm gunner gitriddon yuh lot now. Yawl atter ang-on a sec."

I put my ear against the van wall and listened. For a while I could hear him chopsing with his cronies. I could make some of it out.

"Serves um roit moi ohl boody, thay dinnorter bin thayer unorl."

"We frit em proper. Let em stew frarfowwer, or lunger."

"Neether usenerornamunt me-duck."

As he started to move off, I heard him say that if we tried to leg-it they were to put us in "orspiddle dreckly". The voice faded as he walked away with the rest of them: left us there cold - for time. No door opened on to a new world. It would be over an hour before any doors opened at all. It was the end of the summer, beginning of the backend. The temperature had dropped enough to be uncomfortable. This high pressure would be followed by a depression. We were used to getting pissed on, same old, same old.

Scarpering was out of the question. Of course I thought of loads of ways to escape but what was the point in scattering? Bad man nuh flee. We wanted to be caught. I figure our answers muss have caused the mercenaries some confusion. They weren't sure if they should believe us. They'd seen our equipment though. It turns out that we picked a duff night to go over the wall. Some event was going down. Bigwigs were in the house. Top-bananas with private security guards to stand sentry for them in their crib. Electronic sentinels all around. Earl said, "Maybe, you know, it's like a horror film. Bad shit always happens to man when they skip the blocks, veer out for sticks. That's how it happens in horror films. These pure-breeds in their creepy old house are like Satanists or someting. Their henchmen are taking so long not coz they're calling beast in, but they're calling The Beast up. We're for dinner bruv."

I laughed, but Darren didn't. I wondered about his grip sometimes.

Maybe Earl was right in a way though. Perhaps something nastier than us was in the area. It was taking them a weirdly long time to organise the blue carpet.

"Manz not wrong, I'm feeling it. Horror films blud, you get me? We're trapped in 'ere. I may ave t'goo cannibal t'stay alive. Kna wha I mean?"

I laughed. I realised that Darren was feeling better. He was a survivor, probably at any cost.

"Man have plans to harvest our organs maybe?" Earl suggested helpfully. We fell silent for a few seconds.

Darren spat out what was really on his mind.

"Tall guy init, that walked over t'us man, yeah, before fellaz locked us dain and that - checked us over, teefed our tings. Did you see?"

"See what?" I asked him.

"Man ada gun."

Feet crunched gravel. The door opened. There was the tall man with the piece, lit up by the endless stars gazing down across the dark parkland. He wasn't wearing a uniform. He had on a black suit. The jacket was unbuttoned. Darren was right. He did have some iron. I could make out a holster under his arm: strapped. He rubbed us down again, asked us if we need to piss. He said we could relieve ourselves up the wheels of the van. He checked through our names with us once more. He didn't seem concerned that we might leg it. He didn't sound local - kinda posh. Asked us which of us smoked. Darren held up his hand.

"You can have a smoke. Then you will get back in the vehicle. You will not be here much longer we are just organising matters with the local police."

He handed Darren back his tobacco with his lighter.

"So you're not the police?" I asked.

He didn't respond, began punching info into some kind of handset.

I was quite surprised that he let Darren have a smoke. I guess I was expecting stickler behaviour after our brawl with the others. Darren was clearly under the smoking age too so maybe this guy was all right even if he wouldn't tell us anything.

Darren finished his gasper. He handed back the tobacco with the lighter to Mr Pistol who said, "If you want to commit suicide, it's not my business."

Then he locked us back in the van.

"What did he mean?" Earl asked.

"Not sure, perhaps they're gonna make it look like we topped ourselves. A suicide pact, bruv," said Darren.

"Seen", Earl nodded.

I didn't think so. I thought he was legit. Since I became part-man-part-military-pill my sense of perception iz *da-bomb*. Compared to what it was like time ago, it's zinging. I know a lot more than I used to about what might be going on behind the eyes of other people. It wasn't ESP. It juss seemed to be written on their faces, very clearly. Little things I wouldn't have noticed before. I could tell when people were sad deep down, when they were hiding shit. Samantha picked up on this.

She told me that as part of the legal process I had to take part in a few tests. This was right at the beginning of my time with her on the first day juss after I was unlocked, sprung from the meat-wagon and ASBOed. A muscular bloke with a shaved head had already scrutinized me before the hearing. This baldhead claimed to be a forensic psychologist. There was something not right about him. I didn't think too much about that at the time. Dad turned up with a stoodgie looking brief, distracted me as I finished filling in the last of a few dozen multiple-choice tests in that room in the back of the court building. Darren and Earl were also nearby. We'd been brought there early in the morning. Spent most of the night in a sweatbox that they decanted us into, after about three hours in the back of the security-guards' van. The guys driving the wagon looked like cops. They officially arrested us, took our details then our parents' digits. After removing our laces they made us get into the individual cells. We juss stayed parked up in the grounds of the stately home until dawn. Forced into a foetal position I fell asleep on the small floor as the engine turned over. At least it was warm.

They were barred from my yard. As part of the restrictions of the ASBO I was no longer to associate with Darren or Earl nor they with each other. This meant new schools for two of us. Blouse an' skirts, we could no longer link up. My bredrens' gates were now closed to me. Darren hadn't lost his taste for getting lean though he'd calmed down, stopped messing around with the class A's. His crack-head mates were a pain in the arse always trying to get him to twoc cars. Since we were busted he'd put distance between them. Still he hadn't totally new-leafed, the old one still held an attraction. He would secretly chip round ours to get some greens from Dad. Get red with him, buss some choons. Darren dug retro. Dad liked to keep his ear to the ground; have his finger on the current, take the pulse o' wahgowan. Guess he never grew up. They chilled together regular, broadened each others' horizons. Darren called them ol' skool evenings. I suppose they were in more ways than one. Darren *studied* hard. As he staggered out of the house he was sure to have filed away various licks to nick on a later occasion. I would buck-up on my bredren whatever the ASBO said, meet up town regular. There were a few other rules I was supposed to follow. I was to stay away from the Aristo's stately home, including its immediate surroundings, forever. I was to not write; chat shit about; or broadcast any of the events of the past twenty-four. I was also to have regular meetings with a key-worker. If I broke any of these conditions I would be taken off road, stuck behind bars, and the reporting restrictions – a super-injunction - would still hold.

Later, after I had got all the Behaviour Order bizniz out of the way, I was assigned Samantha as my key-worker. From what I was told was the Youth Offending Team. It was all a bit strange. I was expecting beast, then bang up. It didn't happen like that at all. The whole operation was over in juss one night spent in two vans, and done. I thought it normally took ages to line up that kind of stuff.

A bunch of other man down our road had ASBOs too. Electric Norman caught one. He'd lived on White Lightning since he was about ten. Shtook was a daily occurrence. I liked him - if I checked him early enough. For someone with nothing, who was such a pain in the arse, he was bogglingly generous. Once I asked him to lend me some bus fare - he juss gave it me.

I remember the time he stole a Christmas for Rachel and Eddy. They're a couple or three years younger than me. They live on our block. They've worked hard for years looking after their Mum, Steph, who has MS. A gently intoxicated Norman had turned up at theirs on Christmas Eve in a taxi loaded up with the whole works: turkey; bags and bags of food; a tree; lights; crackers and loads of presents. Helped them do a proper Christmas. No one knew how he'd got the dosh together. The word was that he'd nicked it all – but it was pointless asking Norman, as he had no memory of it. The two large bottles of Advocaat that he treated himself to, at the same time that he got the shopping, eventually wiped his mind clean of all trace of the happy events. Rachel and Eddy would always call him Santa Claus – and he seemed bemused when they did.

He would do anything he could to help people, too much really. Then in the afternoons - after he visited the soup kitchen behind the copshop - the oppressed would return. Limp back the few miles to the estate to submerge, get wankered, go undecipherable; sneering, singing, shouting at ghosts. Wrecked language, absolutely slaughtered, pointless repetitions, dramatic bleats; it went nowhere and neither did he.

I'd have to get away from him if he was too mash-up. He was always in bother. It felt like it took beast ages to actually give him the Behaviour Order; when they finally did, it didn't seem to make much difference to him. The ASBO failed to really get to the crux of his problem. He got hooched-up in a different place, caused ructions elsewhere. Nobody with any power really gave a fuck about him; they juss didn't want him messing with the bookies' customers. He was actually doing some good, profits were down. He hated that shop and what he thought it stood for. His Dad had killed himself over gambling debts. We could have showed the guy some love, but an ASBO was finally issued. I should have remembered wolves tend to come on like shepherds. Norm was right, betting shops smell the carrion in the poor zones and gather. Anyone who can figure out how t'set maths round nex' jugular has got it made: ka-ching ka-ching. In this life lottery more beaten than winners, always. Plenty of saps to sell a dream too and we juss keep buying it. This loser also craved a change in luck. Samantha had my number. At the slightest token of affection I thought I'd hit the jackpot. Brief, intense and irregular: I wasn't able to convert these feelings into anything sensible. She barely seemed to register my nudges in the direction of the big prize. My cherry was on hold: lost heart a flutter. I was addicted to her.

So my plan to be *de' Don Gaagan* had gone a bit a haywire. That morning two cops interrogated me. One of them was quite cute. It only lasted five minutes, which was a shame. They said they were not pressing any charges therefore there was no need for an official interview. The civil courts would deal with all this. Then it was tests; The Beak, and her judgement. She was quite foxy too. I know. I have a problem – awful. It was less obvious to me then. So the Court awarded me my trophy: the ASBO, and then Samantha. Samantha Mir, my beautiful, beautiful ASBO. I was the luckiest body ever to face reporting restrictions.

As long as I could flex with Samantha tings were cook and curry. I didn't check it deep. I didn't check shit. Love is not only blind it has a loose tongue: chatty-chatty whenever I was beside her. I jealously craved her interest. I was monstrously green. I grassed myself. Told her all sorts of bollox - turned infahmah -

snitched on my life. Probably juss as she had predicted on some graph she had drawn up. The pill went unmentioned. No talk about Uncle Vic, at least not until near the end. I held it down. Me nah go deh. She was patient.

After I had kept my appointments with her for a few weeks Sam started visiting me at home. She discussed with Dad the possibility of a visit to what she called a specialist. It was in London. He agreed, probably feeling guilty about giving me the pill; but that was still our secret. Or so I thought. I learned from her that the forensic report Mr Slaphead had written, suggested I might have a kind of attention disorder. This signalled that further tests would be a good idea. Dad probably wanted some reassurance that his application of strong drugs to my food hadn't forever fucked my brain, so he signed up to it. I think he was starting to find the attention of S&M, as he called her, a bit weird; but he went along with it. Soul Mates: that's what I thought it should stand for, but Dad was harder to seduce. It wasn't the same as when he was a yoot. Man would do big time for activities like the foolishness I'd cooked up. A fit Astroturf haired woman, who was too clever by half, shouldn't represent the system. Or at least not be paying so much interes' in us, and so regular. My Dad was ol'skool, thought that probation type people should look ropey, stink of whiskey and miss appointments. Juss having Babylon in the house was bad enough for Dad, so I took the vague paranoia as normal. Helped him clean the vicinity of weed; air the room, tidy up before she came round.

Tests were swiftly organised for me up in the Smoke. The examination was carried out by a couple of white-coated doctors in a private clinic, who looked like they would rather be playing golf. Tanned and fed good, four foreign holidays a year, these guys oozed serious bizniz. One had bad B.O, he minged like rotting onions. Sam called one of the many tests I did an Ekman-procedure. It involved me looking at faces on a screen. These mugs displayed an emotion for fractions of a second then I had to say what the feelings were that were being expressed. I did very well, apparently. S&M told me I had one of the highest scores recorded, ever. Higher than secret service agents; higher than Buddhist monks.

"I see, I shall have to be careful with you," she said.

Be careful we me because I was special? That's what I wanted her to mean. It was partially true, like the second most effective kind of lie. The best are the ones you tell so well you believe them yourself. You are the deceiver and deceived. I convince I. Weave yourself scores of skilful tiny porkies like: me noh craven; I'm an honest geezer. My grey matter would regular spew out streams of self subterfuge:

Mudda Destiny's lips shall smack, smash m' jinx restore deh prince. Mungx toady Dairyleas, dark flavour strong. I see future, I see long. End my days az deh Considerable Cheese, running some tings: shall do whata please.

Used to self-chat bland lyrics like those - constant.

And then there's the huge whoppers you really get wrapped up in like: my life has a meaning beyond what I or some nex' chief may give to it; there is in this blue world someone for everyone; one day my Mum will get back together with my Dad.

Sorted: shit like that used to fog me up, till that tiny pill blasted most of my self-deceptions away. Rinse out. The effect was initially rapid, stark and raw, then gradual - awareness deepened inside over time. Double-face two-dealing and twice minded my past behaviour sliced open clean, my reasonings surgery sharp. I was always plural, my failure to grasp this about myself was where I'd been going wrong. After the medication was popped, when I had recovered, I started to realise that's what most of us manimals are like: self-deluded. I can see it in faces now, hear it in the tone of voices. Tings go easier with lies. People can't take too much reality. Not in this part of the world. Then Samantha came into my life and for a short while the pill's effect was counteracted. It nuh wuk. The insight department turned fully dressback when she hit the area. Dad was right, rudebwoy's brains g'weh, blunted badda dan before 'im dosed.

I had all the symptoms baas - one sick puppy - lovesick puppy, it was obvious. Oblivious to any dog-hearted shenanigans, I obsessed about Samantha, followed her about like a mutt. I could think of little else but there wasn't exactly much thinking involved, more a checking of my new found powers of visualisation. I figure that Sam knew I would eventually suss her out. The tests signalled it. Muss.

They were gathering as much information as they could, trying to figure out how to play me. I even let them take a blood sample - pure folly.

I agreed to that?

Earl was right, wid anyting t'do wid Samantha me wuz as arf-eedjat as nex' man. In the stories people, gods and superheroes have to choose if they will sacrifice their powers for regular human love, but in my case I didn't have a choice. She was human kryptonite. She made my spider senses tingle.

The E-Procedure intrigued me, I googled it. What it had to do with attention problems escaped me. I guess it was the first time in my life I had actually been the best at something. And to be one of the best in whole world - ra! I could ignore Samantha's deeper motives for the tests, but there was a time in that swish clinic when I started to feel edgy. Uneasy in a way that began to grow as time went on - however much I might have denied it to Darren and Dad.

It was when B.O Joe, the white coated stinking bastard with a stoosh watch, looked at the results. For a fraction of a second as he saw some implications, he stared up at my face.

I could tell that he was now terrified of me. He did his best to hide it. I began to suspect maybe tests weren't such a good idea. I didn't want Dad to get in trouble. I had never really frightened anyone like that before. Even for juss a thousandth of a second that it registered. Earl would have loved it - bless. I wanted to know what could make someone look at me like that, but I wasn't in a hurry. I suppose later I found out. My intense hormones constantly distracted me, kept me in a bit of frenzy. Though I doubted Samantha would have an attraction to me in that way, a boy can dream. Regular bashment - that was an answer.

By this time I was already too rampantly obsessed with the delights of Ms Mir to be worrying about the fact that I had not ended up in a Secure Unit. Both Dad and Darren had beautiful suspicious weed filled minds, full of blazing nous. Later they would become full-blown paranoid by most standards. Still, 'xtra sensi perceptions can be useful. I had my focus on other more voluptuous areas. ASBO: what a lovely word, it was a license to stalk and talk. Sam was fit. I loved speaking with her. It was weird. I grilled her hard about this, that and the other. We discussed the ins-and-outs of every cat's arse that might throw some shine on the cloudy nature of shit, some overstanding of the festering fakeness all-n-sundry munched. We chatted about my life, my dreams and my hopes. She told me about some of hers, they may have been real. But my lie-dar was unplugged as far as she was concerned. So I don't know. Whatever was the truth, there was never really much in the way of *lite* conversation with Samantha. In fairness to her, and my badself, I think she liked me too. Or it is possible that this is an example of the best kind of lie, which the pill has yet to help me realise and let go. Perhaps Samantha was attracted to what the pill could do. It doesn't really matter now. However much she may have liked me, she was still playing me like poker. In this venture some nameless military outfit staked her. I was a trapping bet. Bait. These man gambled on drawing Vic to their stakeout. I wager they might also have been planning to join me up, have me kept under their control on some base in Greenland or somet'ing. For the time being maybe they could kill to two buds with the same stoner: draw Vic back to Dad's. I feel that getting me to take the shilling was Samantha's ultimate task, which she was slowly performing for boardroom spooks, duppy generals. I see this now in some of the stuff we did together. The visit to the air show; the flight in the Apache; the books she got me to read.

Now I think back I suppose it was probably those first tests I did with the peelhead. They muss have calculated I would bond with an older woman, that I had a need to connect with one; that this was somehow linked up with my crime. It was my crooked mind that cooked up the idea to exhume the Princess's body, though my buddies did not grass. They each said that they had thought of it. When the chips were down, my crew stuck tru'. Darren and Earl, my gang-stars: my stars. Of course they wanted to be the notorious badman. I felt a bit stink being so shady and cold with my bredren and dragging them into this foolishness, see it deh. Anyway, it turned out okay. I didn't run all twisted too long. Sam appeared, took my mind off of it. The headshrinkers muss have sussed me straight off. Earl and Darren weren't placed on such a tight programme. They were quite lucky. Earl stayed at school got into a sports scheme, talked about opening up a gym one day and Darren was enrolled onto a sound engineering course. They both really started to blossom. All down to the intervention of agencies unknown, who for the purpose of dealing with me were calling themselves the Youth Offending Team. Maybe in their case it actually was the YOT lot. So far it had worked out okay for my breh. Who says crime doesn't pay? Tell that to the people who own the private jails where they kept my Dad. It was a cover-up where nearly everyone was happy - for a while. I guess they were right on target. Their psychological predictions validated. I was pathetically fascinated with Samantha. She moved like gravity could not confine her. Her smart-arse silence ripped the vicinity like a stun-grenade. With Samantha, it was always what she didn't say.

Eyes I wouldn't recognise had looked at my behaviour, my history. They studied me far deeper than I realised. I was too in love to clearly see it, Ekman powers, or not. My name muss have been on a list to alert the bully, or perhaps they were bugging our house even back before we were busted. It was Vic they wanted. I was a kind of bonus prize.

Juss when I needed more of Dad's attention with some time to think, his little angel bailed from her Mum's on the Eastern District - moved in with us. My half-sister Fiona: Fi, the Babybrat from Bellinge. Whoever named that place was having a laugh. Fi was carrying on going to school over there, so I had some time when she wasn't around. Checking the Eastern Bloc was a bit of a mission - two bus journeys. That district had changed a lot over the years. Dad said plenty people vamp Poland and Lithuanian sides decamped in them endz now - hard workin' for gherkin and kebahsa. When Dad was a kid, man were pointing nukes at us - original. Now trekked distance, parked here, got a ticket, brought into our zlotyree - often ear'ole fellas jawing Polski.

Our cold war skirmishes are between different postcodes - mindless. It doesn't really matter what your origins are it's the turf you represent, like Première League football teams.

Jan was one of my spars, known him from long time at school. His folks chipped with him here, from Poland, when we were in infants. His Dad started off driving coaches, ended up working down Carlsberg. His Mum worked over at Barclaycard. Both those buildings looked liked different kinds of spacecraft piloted by rival creatures that had landed here to mine on some kind of evil energy crystals. Northampton has always traded in souls, but in "olden- toimes" they were largely juss on the bottom of your feet. Immortal debt with the means to forget about it, that's what the town exported while I was growing up. That's our own double special brew. Impossible dreams and burst bubbles: make money either way. Back in lower skool dayz Jan and me used to teef the beer his Dad got from work. We'd take it over the woods, throw the empties at the trains. They had their own kind of brand, juss for the workers. Tasted nicer than any of the stuff they sold, or may be it's juss that stolen beer tastes better. Beer doesn't exactly taste too tough anyway; it's like everything else, you have to learn it. Big and clever, that's what we wanted to be back then I suppose. But after a while, all I wanted to be was big. Then I was spiked. I lost the taste for brew totally - became cleverer than I had ever imagined it was possible to be. Weird to think if it had turned out different, before we were even born Jan's folks' country and mine could have ended along with the lives of everyone in them. No wonder my old man turned to weed. There's a statue in Abington Street that Dad used to call, *The Four-minute Warning*. Metal children flee, frozen in panic, on top of a giant shoe-making tool. Gran called it a "last." The Last People, what's that all about? A gravestone to long lost jobs. Why plant that in Abington Street, right in the middle of the town centre? I'm really surprised someone hasn't half-inched it, melted the fucker down for coin. What the frigg was the point of a four-minute warning anyway? Wonder what panic plans people had in place should them hear the sound of sirens? How did they manage to sell it as a good ting? An English goodbye - juss about time for a last cup of tea; juss don't put too much water in the kettle. How would you like to spend your last four, in ignorance of the oncoming fireball never even hearing the explosion; or filled with panic and fear, heart beating to burst like a star-shell over an air-raid warning soundtrack? Since I awoke from my life before the pill, I can see it clear: fear makes us gullible. It turns off most off the brain gubbins that makes us proper human - standard. The wolves still at that shit. Same game different name. Decided not to listen, flicked the channel, was bored of being told who my enemies were - constant. I would pick my own. Fight my own war. Be my own shepherd. Fuck the Government. Fuck all Governments.

The flight in the Apache was the bizniz though.

Anger can turn your wits to shit too, I suppose.

Jan's folks were very strict, religious. He had to go to special Polish school on Saturdays, used to feel stink about it. I met him on the bus after my sister had moved in. Bucked-up on Fi up town while getting some supplies for a project I was working on. I bumped into her, literally, was so lost in thought. She was vex. I'd made her look 'xtra in front of Jan - scuffed her favourite shoes. No fear they'd been made in Northampton, they weren't even leather. Unlike the Goths that were milling around us who didn't seem to wear much else. They looked dangerous, but were quite placid. It seemed that it was always the same types, who wanted to stand around at the top of Abington Street in black clothes wearing make-up and a face full of metal. Immortals? Perhaps it was some kind of shrine. They were there when I was a kid. It couldn't be the same people. Dad said they started appearing when he was a yoot. Tribes, what makes them come and go? Dad talked about skinheads. I've never seen one in the flesh, though I have seen a Teddy boy in the bus station. He looked older than time. He'd kept the look his whole life. Tatts look rough on really old folk. This geezer had ink on the blink - serious. His quiff wasn't too clever; more of juss an arse, than a duck's arse. But he was a Ted. He was frozen as a Ted. I wonder how the Goths would react if I could wave my finger, suddenly make them seventy five years old? That would be jokes. Jan had gothic emo-ish tendencies. Nothing too heavy, else his folks would freak out. I guess that was part of the idea. He explored the borderline, with eye-liner. We walked up through the piss alley at the back of the market square, got the bus back together. Fi clearly had designs on Jan. Suited me - if I could link her up with him then I'd have more time to flex. The god-fearing folks might be a problem, with Fiona being a few years younger than him and not exactly church material. I wasn't specifically chupid cupid - juss lending a hand to nature, so she could take her course directly. I'd seen it clear on their faces. It would only be a mater of time. Jan could cotch round our yard nuff time he liked, as long as he kept my sister out of any botheration aimed in my direction.

Dad wasn't a good role model in the birth control department, when he was younger he couldn't keep it in his pants. Regular coxman, if he were to be believed. Wouldn't be surprised to find out I had a whole load of brothers and sisters other than Fiona. She was a bit of a pain. It wasn't that I didn't like her, I did. I do. It's juss that she always wanted to ease-up with me. Whatever I was doing, she wanted to do it too. Hanging with a thirteen-year-old girl is not my ting for regular time killing activities, and I didn't fancy any of her mates. Jan and Fi had this bizarre interest in common they both were into musicals. I don't know why. They both juss used to get off on gawping at them together. They weren't really my scene, though a martial arts musical might be worth watching. I like the idea of people karate kicking the shit out of each other in mid air, while singing their lungs loose - something for everybody.

Perhaps I should write one based on my posse's run in with the watchmen and our quest for ill repute. Darren could do the choons. We could call it; *Beasties and the Beaut*, or perhaps; *The Princess and the P.* Those lyrics swerved a little towards the panto side, perhaps I should emphasise the fighting. Maybe *Furious Fists of Funk* would be more Earl-esque. I would like to do this scene where there would be a sweatbox made out of clear bullet-proof glass and we would be being driven in it through Northampton. Each of the badman kickin' it, chillin' in our little glass cell emitting lyrics and looking nuff ruff, tuff and buff - while the people lined the streets and screamed. As we went past on our way to face the music, they would pitch rotten veg, fling eggs and lob insults in a perfectly choreographed way. We would ignore them, protected behind the glass force field, as we demonstrate improbably hard kung-fu style dance moves. Dad couldn't stand musicals. Hell had come to our house, but whatever for Fiona. My old man would go about his tings then come back late enough to say it was bedtime as soon as he rocked up. Usually he'd juss be hanging with his spar Isaac or round at Gran's.

Jan and Fi were into old, new, and foreign stuff as long as it had singing in it. They loved anything from Bollywood, *South Park*, *Eight Mile*, *The Jungle Book* - even dash on the *Sound of Musack.* I liked a really really ancient one, with this geezer called Zinga who worked in some docks and who then becomes a singer, then a king, reminded me a bit of Vic. I think Gran's Mum had been into the truly old ones - Gran 'membered dem from long time. Fiona downloaded some to show to Gran on the mobile. I wondered what it was they found so compelling about people bursting into song.

I was spending a lot of time reading. I went to the library nearly every day. I'd never been there much until I was pilled-up. I would obsess about all sorts so I guess I related to Fi and Jan's odd hobby. My fixations were partially fuelled by Samantha, partly by my own badmind. Fi didn't know about the pill. She teased me saying that I had been "nerd gassed".

Most people quickly forget about a change, juss accept it. With others it took longer. The local team troops didn't give me any grief, after I dealt with the dickhead - Tovey. It was pretty soon after I shed my previous skin. He saw me reading a book on genetic engineering outside my gates. He decided t'mess. The scroat rushed up, stepped to me, took the book out my hands, and smashed me in my boat in front of all the main faces: urgent to quell any learning insurgency. It was juss so much roach-material to him - he didn't know jack. Bloody hell my whole head seemed to ring. It stung like when a football hits you on the cheek in the rain. There was no way a wasteman was going to bwoy me up. Committed to the crime of books, that's me right there. I held it down, wanted to wait for the right moment. Can't deny I had an instant urge to cut his pipes with a library card. I'd return it later. He'd pay the fine. So nex' day when I spied Tovey in front of all dem gang-man near the green, I called him over.

"Ever meddle with me again muppet," I whispered, "you'll get some more."

He leaned in to hear me. I hit him in the chest with a massive jolt from a homemade stun-gun I'd been dabbling with. Seemed it worked fine - that's my kind of pause button.

"Man needed t' learn. Books, deh way forward." I yelled so all the boys would hear. As he twitched on the floor Tovey was actually frothing at the mouth - impressive - may have been electronically induced epilepsy. They say his heart stopped, the medics in the ambulance brought him back round. For a while, I had killed him. Well that was the word. My props went up even more after that. Shame that it wasn't even captured on a mobile, but probably juss as well for me. Duggy, who was sort of that crew's General, thought it was really funny. He always called me Sparkz after that and made it known, it was nang. He didn't take it personal - Tovey was a tosser he had it coming. Could be that he was wary of a taste of my 'lectrickery, no doubt that Duggy also sort of saw it as a product demonstration that I'd laid on for him. So it was all okay. Dug was alright really, he'd managed to avoid getting sent down - even though he'd been excluded from education for ages. That's pretty much a prison sentence - in the end. So he muss have had some smarts to have stayed out of the clutches of the filth, even if the various schools he'd been lobbed out of had failed to find any constructive use for them. He wanted me to make him a weapon like mine.

I said, "Sure, I think I could do one that was better".

Probably put them into the care of some year sevens. That's the way it was going: younger and younger. No one squealed to the authorities, but people don't tend to round our end. Bad shit happens. There are a few families you don't want to get on the wrong side of, ours might be one - come to think. Once he'd recovered Tovey never gave me bother again. Funny thing was, not long after I saw him reading a novel. I think it may have been what the shrinkers call, Pavlovian training. No one hassled me, even though I'd wandered around carrying books. No longer bothered with the games of baiting the police, or standing around for hours doing fuckall, I was probably also safe coz of Dad. There was some bizniz shit going down between my old man and the crew that I didn't want to know about. And perhaps something else had happened to me that they instinctively knew to steer clear of. Either way, I got surprising little hassle, even when they'd been on the brew.

Generally I chilled with Fi and Jan in the room. I focused so much on the ideas I was scanning, I forgot about the musicals. Lyrics kind of leaked into me, round the sides. I discovered the M.I.T site where their course materials are available to all. Free access to one of the best colleges in world, the Massachusetts Institute of Technology, without ever leaving the room - cheers! So I started trying to fathom the mysteries of nature, one at a time. One night it was neuroscience; the nex', film studies. I opened my mind, into it I poured information. I asked myself more and more questions, began to realise that I knew zippo about anything. Even with military-chemical assistance there was a lot of shit that would remain beyond my reach unless we can extend the human life span by a factor of ten, or so. It was not possible for one person to have a working understanding of every area of study any more. I knew I knew fuckall and maybe only ever could know fuck-all, but at least I knew that; and that was an improvement. Still, I was having fun. They say a little knowledge is dangerous. I hoped so.

After I had been seeing her for a couple of weeks, Samantha got me to read a whole bunch of books. First it was literature. She gave me about forty paperbacks, told me to read them. I checked them over a weekend. It didn't take me very long. The most time I spent was in looking up words. I made sure I knew what they meant. In the end I decided to juss read the whole of the dictionary as well. I'd lifted one from Smith's. There's some pretty weird information in a dictionary, more of a story than you might think. It's probably my favourite book. Inglish slanguage, one big mash up – cool yeah. Hidden meanings in the texture, words robbed from everywhere – international piracy. Mixed and transformed like we all are here, constant battles over the changes; always shifting, always twisting. Your vocabulary is an arsenal it should have as many weapons as possible – you need to know how to change the armaments to fit the circumstances.

The following week she gave me a test. She said that my results were impressive for my age. I was around the level of a graduate student, so I was about five years ahead. Not bad for a weekend spent reading. She was wicked at bigging me up. Like the Roman poet that she got me to read says, *They can do all because they think they can*. With these results in mind, she said that they thought I needed to attend a place with particular facilities and specialists, because of my alleged attention problem. The only attention problem that I could see that I had was that I didn't get enough of the kind I wanted.

It so happened that a place had become available up at an experimental school which had only recently opened out on the Welford Road. A special school for his gifted son, Dad was always going to say yes to that. It was what he had always wanted and it was coming true before his eyes. One good point about the school was that I could get there across the fields. That autumn I crossed the railway, then the foggy Nenn, every weekday morning at exactly the same time - juss after the red and grey Virgin train went past. It's a good job that I had not been banned from all of the nob's lands, else I would practically never have been able to leave my home.

The so-called school was a modified detached house, older than our yard but a lot bigger, built out of bright orange bricks. From its garden you could see towards the river and the woods. To the left, in the distance, was what looked like a concrete coloured lighthouse. It was as far away from the sea as it possible to be in England - perhaps it was an echo of the future. This tower, in Jimmy's End, was all that remained of Express Lifts where Darren's Dad used to work before we were born. He used to rant on that those were the days when a man could go for a jar with his mates after doing hard manual work all day long; then go watch the Cobblers together on weekends in the old stadium near Abington Park where you had to stand up, and stand your ground. No namby pamby sitting on your numb arse like a numpty. It sounded like a nightmare to me - a naff one. His mind had got stuck between two floors. No one would ever come to rescue him. When I was a kid, I used to imagine that the tower was a rocket. That the doorway to outer space was juss down the road. I began the countdown to the day I would be launched in it. I wonder what it is about this Earth that meant that as soon as my brain had developed enough to think about what I could do here on this planet, it decided the best track would be to become someone with the power to leave. Not juss the estate, but the whole fucking world. It wasn't as if I was the only one with that idea, wanting to be an astronaut is a mouldering chestnut. Perhaps I should put this forward as a new psychological theory, shrinkers might call it something like *the stage of initial infant clarity,* which I strongly suspect most children pass through.

It was when I started messing with the explosives that I remembered my rocket-powered dreams. Missiles were an interesting problem, but I resisted the urge to talk to my teachers about them. I only had two. Mr Edwards and Mr Rahiman. They came on more like shinkers than teachers, and perhaps they were. I did see about seven other students there over the weeks. They were clearly all Fraggles. Place wasn't exactly ram, no one else appeared to go there all the time like I did. I guess I was lucky. They could have juss nutted me off; sectioned me; stuck me in a bin.

To start off with it was fun, lots of one-to-one with intelligent people in a bright airy place where the focus was me. The workers there were difficult to read, like they were defending themselves somehow. Raihman hid behind his beard; came on like a silent sulking granite-faced pie-lover, who projected having juss two emotions - nothing and screwface. The only time I think that he got really pissed off for real was when he lost a game of Go, which he played relentlessly over the internet like an addiction. He tried to get me into it. He showed me the rules. I beat him three games in a row. He stopped mentioning it. The perpetually smooth face of Edwards on the other hand always came over a little too jovial. He was kind of funny, thin with a vast round head and big feet, like someone had deprived him of light then forced him to grow. He told me stories about Iraq in the first Gulf war. Both these dudes carried on like they were ex-military. I didn't make anything of that at the time. Raihman said he originally trained as a doctor, had been a medic in Iraq - before turning to specialised teaching. I thought I saw him smile, briefly, when he told me that. Edwards said that he'd been involved in the organisation of supplies. Often the conversation would drift into matters military. This was intentional of course, though they did it well. I didn't notice any tell tale emotions on either of their faces at the time.

The house was a lot better than school plus Samantha put in regular appearances to sugar the pill. She would take me out on day trips. I could go about two minutes without thinking about her. I don't know how I got anything done at all. For a few weeks I almost ran there every day, did whatever they asked me to do. More than general lessons, I enjoyed what I called

PeSt and the tutors called *Personal Study*. They were probably being ironic.

PeSt meant I had to think, research, read a bunch of books; sometimes run an experiment; write or make a ting; surf; calculate - whatever. Every few days I had to give a report to the tutor on what I had been doing. In those few weeks I wrote more than I'd ever written before. I took charge of myself. I wanted to do it. No one had to ask me. All the years of school damage had been suddenly cleansed. It was like when I first went to school, when I was still a keen nipper, but now with adult skills. The stuff I had been thinking about they would really go into it with me - make a few suggestions then off I'd go again. I am sure they analysed me as I studied. I wonder what they made of the various crap I immersed myself in. They seemed particularly curious when I started to show an interest in anything to do with military history or training. That's because they were into it.

It was through this process that I became aware of the amazing stuff you can do at home. I got into reactions, all kinds of reactions. What were reactions? I thought about different types: physical, chemical, emotional. There's nothing more important than chemistry. I began to do small-scale experiments. I'd make stuff in our tiny shed. It was time consuming grinding up the metals, but they were easy enough to find. Thermite was clearly my most promising creation, as I could develop it relatively silently, it wouldn't necessarily explode if it went off by accident.

Pure incendiary, two and a half thousand degrees, it would melt clean through steel. Once it was going there was no way to stop it, it would work underwater. Aluminium lusts for the oxygen in the rust, and the rust has to be coaxed into letting its O go. The result molten iron. Beauty. It was brilliant stuff. I found a way of triggering the process using sparklers. I was looking to use it to evaporate locks, wanted to get back into my old school one night: rinse their chemistry supplies. I figured out that it might get me into the store cupboard, which was pretty much armoured. It was difficult shit to apply. I messed about in the hut with ways of getting it to stick to stuff, rather than juss be loose powder. My self-defence mechanism stopped me from mentioning this hobby to people at the new school; in fact I didn't mention it to anyone. I reckon that's the only way to go, the amount of Dad's mates who went down coz they blabbed t'nex' man is amazing. "Wenchman, sprat an' mackaba should keep him mout shut, him would neva get kech."

Dad's ancient wisdom was obviously pre-net.

Though Dad knew I was up to something, he kept his head low. Once he saw me testing a bucky flame-thrower that I had adapted from a giant water pistol. I reckon that Duggy would have taken quite a few off of me, if he'd have known about them. I could tell that it took Dad all his will power to not ask me to let him have a go on it. He was mashed. I pestered him to try it. He laughed and said, "ASBO bwoy bring bully roun't'gates nuff time areddi." He tried to keep his serious face on. "Our yoot busy wid strong plans, gonna end itarl; commit beast'icide?" He let the words linger.

Then in a louder voice he said, "Throw out deh weapon." He looked at me straight, "Itching digits, brains all mash-up on deh floor. See it dere." He put his hands in the air as if pointing a rifle, squinted one eye, squeezed an imaginary trigger.

"Last ting before darkness, yuh ear deh shot. Game over. Ya c'yaan 'ear, ya muss feel."

He was right. Surprisingly forward thinking for my old man. It was too successful - massive jets of fire. I was likely to end up appearing in the scopes of the Armed Response Unit, lit good; heading for a fatal dose of laser beam measles or a tazer up my arse. I decided I would stash the pistol at Earl's for the time being, in case anyone else had seen me with it. I put my faith in thermite, continued with my quieter experiments, began to change my focus. I should use my noggin to bring in a large amount of readies, in the quickest possible time. Could buy all the weapons I might need then.

I spoke to Mum on the phone. She had said that she was coming to Northampton to see me at the weekend. I hadn't seen her since I was captured. I'd only spoken to her once since then.

On the same day as I spoke to Mum I had one of my trips away from the school. Samantha drove me to the Church of St Mary the Virgin at Great Brington where Dad had said the Princess was really buried. It was juss on the edge of the area I was allowed into. I wouldn't have been able to get there by walking along the bridleway, as I would have had to cross too close to the toffs' yard. The sandstone church was pretty much the nearest building to the stately home. In fact I was probably breaking the Order but Sam didn't seem bothered. She didn't mention Dad's conspiracy theory about the Princess really being in there. Perhaps she took me there as a way of trying to make me think about the consequences of my actions on the family. I don't know. She came on like we juss happened to be passing it. I didn't bring the rumours up either, I was seduced by the idea of my "new life" at the school. I didn't want to remind her of how she knew me. It was foolishness, how was she going to forget? I was actually interested in local history at that point. Well I was attracted by whatever Samantha was into. We stopped in at the church so that she could explain something about it to me. Perhaps it was her idea of a joke and the Princess really was buried in there. Anything was possible. According to Sam it was rumoured that Queen Mary's head was under the altar, though she didn't believe it herself. I asked her what god they were worshipping in there and she laughed nervously, "The usual one."

She said architecture was one of her delights, the wedding of science and art was what did it for her.

This was a lovely church, one of her favourites. It wasn't as special as four or five other churches in the area that she mentioned, including St Peter's and Sep's church in the town centre. For her though, this was a wonderful place. Sam's family had ancient links to the area. Nineteen generations of the Princess's ancestors were buried in there too, apparently. When she told me that, Dad's theory started to sound more plausible. Why would they stick her in a swampy pet cemetery when they could stick her here?

Red rusting leaves dropped in the sunlight, natural confetti. She traced her finger around the carvings on her ancestor's stone. Covered in carroty lichens, it was dead old, a slightly orange cheese that flaked and crumbled. The gravestone was forgetting what it was. It had Alzheimer's, you could hardly read it.

She obviously was really into the vibe of the place. It was so quiet. It was hard to believe we were close to my gates. We spent nearly two uninterrupted hours in the church chatting shit. I think it was the first time I had enjoyed being in a church. She decoded a bit of it for me, told me some of the history of the building. As we walked in through the porch, I saw the ancient chunky wooden door like a castle's. I was struck with the thought that this place was originally perched here on the edge of the hill for military reasons. I had the army on the brain that day.

"You're probably right about that. Brington is said to mean town on the brink. You get quite a view from here. Good place for a beacon."

I told her that boiling oil might come in handy if you needed to defend a large tower on a hill. Later I was to modify my opinion.

Sam opened the door. We stepped into the aisle. It was quiet. The stained glass window at the back looked like an enormous advent calendar, the kind without chocolates. William Morris made it. Sam said he was an important artist about a hundred years ago. I made a note to Wiki-p him at some point. Thirteen glowing figures had their backs to me. They stood looking at a lamb that was standing forever behind a magnificent blue sky. The sheep held the George's cross. I knew it was probably symbolic of something religious. No prizes for guessing that. A sheep holding the English flag seemed about right to me. The message I was getting from it probably wasn't one he had in mind when he made it. Guess William Morris has never had a BNP leaflet stuck through his door.

Samantha showed me a coat-of-arms carved onto the end of a bench, which explained the special relationship between Americans and this church and why the US flag was flying outside of it. It was a crest of stars and stripes. She said it belonged to the Washington family. The ancestors of George Washington had lived here and were buried here. It was funny how this ancient family crest, carved long before the Washingtons had set out for America, was basically the Union Flag; Old Glory; The Stars and Stripes. The same as was fluttering in the breeze outside. I'm sure Dad would have something to say about that. He would occasionally rant that since the year dot the same families have had it all sewn up. If he'd been toking too hard he'd start gobbing on about the Masons as well. He drew the line at lizard people, he thought that was silly. Sometime's he said he was almost glad he couldn't read too well.

Darren's Dad told me about the lizard people yonks ago. He'd been to a talk. This guy that used to be a goalkeeper, I think that might have been part of the appeal, took his money off him, then told him that the prime seed people who are running tings are actually 'xtra-terrestrial reptiles - for real. Then he rinsed him of some more dosh and gave him a book. He told me that he'd read it all. He was now convinced that every bit of it was true, the lizard people called the shots. This was back before I could be bothered to read too much, so I juss remember the cover. I had some sense even before the pill. I can recall staring in to the sparkling reptile eyes thinking if Darren's Dad really believes that these creatures are in charge why is he so calmly telling me about it and not organising a fight back? Why isn't *The Keeper* organising a fight back? It was weird. All Darren's Dad's mates were into it, and they said they believed it. When I asked them, "What do you plan to do about it then?" Somehow they didn't seem to be bothered. It was like a virus, they wanted to convince you it was true but they didn't want you to do anything about it. I didn't get it. Unless it's a strange adaptation of goal keeping; defending by standing out in the open, narrowing the angles. Perhaps *The Keeper* is a lizard himself. He turns any potential threats to *lizardkind* in to dribbling zombies who will mindlessly shell out to attend meetings to learn more. End up pacified by a special lizard toxin that he farts out of his mouth as he talks. That's what gets them all transfixed enough to fling down more dosh, then talk and talk about lizards rather than offing them. When last year Darren started banging on about it too, that's what I told him had happened to his Dad. Sometimes, I thought Darren might lose it. "He's been knobbled," I told him. "Now it's up to you to save him."

"Fuck that," he said.

Classic Darren - quality. Always hustling. Turned out he didn't really give a toss about an E.T invasion. He juss thought there might be mileage in it somewhere, even if it were true. Perhaps do a choon about the lizards that's the kind of issue that needs a funky soundtrack. A theme night for a club: fly the lizard mother-ship right to the mother lode. He'd have a hit and sell reptile repellent on the back of it, or someting.

If *The Keeper* was to be believed then this church was probably some kind of cold blooded shrine. To Sam it was more like a big book that she could read.

In the left hand corner there was a weird fenced off zone. It was alarmed, according to a warning sign. This shrine was painted a blue that seemed to be both a light and dark shade simultaneously. The colour of their blood I suppose. There were obelisks with other symbolic stuff - you could see some of it through the screen but you weren't allowed in. Sam didn't have a key, or so she said. Dad's theory seemed highly plausible. The Princess probably was buried in there. I didn't really care. I was so rapt, wrapped up in what that ravishing raptor was telling me. She was going to get me some *Trust* money, to pay for me to go to University a few years earlier than normal. She assured me that she would give me a ring in two days, to sort out taking me to visit this Trust where I had to give a talk about why I needed the money. Hand in hand with this she promised to guide me in thinking about what I would need to say to this organisation.

I almost danced around the church. She would give me directions. I would join her at an Office. It was as good as in the bank. The church is the only witness to this. It seems to be a popular location for big lies. She was grooming me. Vic was her man. Then as we left the church, walked back to the car, she dropped it in the phrase, *"in exchange"*.

After she had said that she would do it. Almost as an afterthought, she named her percentage. All I had to do was to give her a ring if I heard anything about a known criminal. If I knew anything now I was to speak now, nothing wrong with that. It was what was right.

That's what she'd been asked to tell me. She didn't say who was pulling her strings. I didn't ask. I had gone cold. I remembered a vow to Dad, to say nothing about Vic to anyone. I remained quiet. Sam looked at me as if sizing me up then walked towards her car.

"My Dear, you can take the boy out of the street but you can't take the street out of the boy. You are not an informer. You'll be undercover. They will catch him anyway and, with your help, less people may be hurt."

She moved her hand to her bag took out a bottle of scent squirted herself a few times. Then put it back. She took out her car keys. I didn't like the sound of any people being hurt. I thought about Dad. I thought about Mum.

I felt myself about to say, "Yes".

Then my brain kinda seized up.

"Take me home," I said, "I'll let you know."

I think there may have been something in the spray designed to mess with my oxytocin levels. I don't have any evidence of this other than the look on her face as she sprayed it. And the feelings, when I thought about it, that I could remember from the other times that I smelled that smell. I've come to understand that *The Power* have that kind of shit to hand.

I should have stolen some while I had the chance.

When I got back in, Dad said that Mum had rung and cancelled.

He looked at me sadly as I kissed teeth; shouldn't have got my hopes up, chu. I felt like exploding. I didn't want to think about it. I juss wanted to go to bed. Dad tried to be nice. I wanted to lie down, sulk for a while. He said, "Time longer than string, she'll reach, tings nuh wuk out dis time. Y'Mudda loves er likkle picney. She juss ill".

He looked at me again, I could see that's what he wanted to believe but he was having difficulty. Dad used his classic change the subject routine. It often got results. Out of the blue, a bit too loud to be normal, he said, "Wonder how Victor's hustling out on dem SOLOMON ISLANDS?"

I looked at him funny, then twigged. He never called him Victor. I pointed to my ear, then at the wall. He nodded slowly. He'd been burning too hard, gone paranoid. He moved his first two fingers like a walking man. I nodded. I said, "I'm sure he's having a great time in the SOLOMON ISLANDS Dad." Then as I followed my old man out of the house in to the dark, I added juss for a laugh, "He's worth trillions by now. What with *the deal* and everything."

Dad muss have picked the islands at random, probably a half remembered fragment from one the nature programs he liked to watch when cained to the max. Once we got outside my eyes adjusted to the dusk. We then put distance between us and the yard. He

65

told me he had no idea where Vic was. If he was right we'd soon be getting a visit from someone. I didn't tell him about Samantha's proposal. I was still in denial. He told me how to get in touch with Vic though - only to be used in an emergency. I had to get a BlackBerry first. No problem.

We walked down towards the Nenn, where Dad used to walk with me when I was a kid. He'd go pick magic mushies on the fields near the farm. Dad told me that it was here that he fessed-up to Darren about Vic and the pill. That morning he was out teaching D how to identify Liberty Caps. They pop out of the green, the colour of bone, rubbery little hats with nipples on the end - junjos. I used to collect them with him. They were sacred too apparently. It didn't stop Dad banging them out this time of year. I don't think Dad took them very often, one of his yoot tings. Probably getting too lazy to go pick them every morning, so he had decided to franchise out his little operation to the nex' generation. He knew I wouldn't be into it. I had taken a turn for the puritanical since he spiked me, so I wasn't going to juggle them. Darren was always one for a business opportunity. He could shot out the shrooms to his spars on the music course.

Darren had apparently bucked up on Dad in town then they headed for the fields together. Daz had been for his regular assessment meeting with the do-gooders along the Billing Road. One of the YOT crew had let a few tings slip that had induced our Darren to believe that someone muss be bugging our yard - information that Dad was always ripe to believe. (Believe.)

That's what Dad told me eventually after going off at a tangent again about Darren's slack mushroom finding skills. Daz hadn't been much cop at telling the difference between the tiny little mushies that grew near the railway line. He didn't like "the countryside", he told Dad. It was only a few hundred yards away from his gates. The couple of horses in the field spooked him. He was screwing about grass eating vermin, as his foot fell into an old wasp nest that was in a hole in the ground. There weren't even any wasps, but that was enough for Darren. He cussed Dad off, told him he could suck out - and jacked it in. Dad creased up as he told me about it.

Instead they walked off round the woods, went twos on a J.

Large mushrooms were growing along the path into the woods under a silver birch. Dad identified the species. He juss stopped Darren from crushing their fairy-ring. They were a red and white spotted type toadstool that Dad called, *The Berserker*. He liked the name, and so did I.

"Tings not even banned." He said almost as if he were disappointed. For Dad legalisation would take some of the money and a lot of fun out of drugs.

I asked him, how did he know so much without reading? He told me that he had learned about them during his version of going to college: while doing bird in a local. An old pad-mate of his told him about them, but he'd never found one before. He'd taken them though, swapped some of his canteen for them, went totally bananas with his co-d - ended up in Segregation.

Dad was impressed with them largely it seemed because his behaviour on them had increased his rep out on the landings, made people a bit more wary of him. That was the way he liked to roll while banged-up. He was also tickled by them because they hadn't shown up in a piss-test that he'd had to take after the incident. This made him laugh, as he said one of the tings about this mushroom is it's in the piss of people who take it. You can get mash-up drinking their piss.

He said no dog is gonna sniff out the piss in the bog during a pad-spin: don't flush, drink later. Even in Seg' he could get high. I thought it was rank, he was a whole bag of nastiness. Dad said prison was prison, and you'd be surprised what people will pay for. He told me some man thought that the Vikings used this fungus to get themselves into killing rages. Dad didn't think tripping troops would be too effective. Berserking is a ting you do on your own, was his opinion.

"Spot on," he said, "'it deh spot", as he showed me the one he had kept. The red skin was thin and waxy. It split in large dots, revealing the white flesh underneath – it smelt *wrong*.

D had plans to shot out the rest of the crop. I wondered what results that might have on the Music Department. Dad didn't need mushrooms to go paranoid I didn't need them to run amok. He told me that Darren had said that during his meeting in town with the Authorities, a grizzly fucker had told him that he knew Darren was hanging out at our house in breech of the ASBO; that this was his final warning; anymore violations he'd loose his place on the music course - end up in a Secure Unit.

How could they know? He came to ours hoodied-up, never even carried his mobile. And he had told no one, except Earl, who was no grass. Darren would never dare to fling accusations at Earl. So they muss be listening in was Daz's conclusion.

"Why would man be dain buggin yer yard, init? Sussed yer fer summut big? Could be a Judas in yer yard." Darren quizzed Dad hard, apparently.

Dad could do a pretty funny impression of Darren he exaggerated Daz's Northampton twang, made him sound like the guy who locked us in the Van. The other people there the night Darren came over were, Fi, Jan and me. So it was unlikely one of us had snitched. None of those man would turn reporter, traitor, nark. Even though Darren often got on Jan's case, Jan wouldn't grass him up. Darren made Dad laugh. Even Dad wasn't that paranoid.

So that's when he told him about Uncle Vic and his pill: squared with him about a possible reason. They

69

were spars after all. I think Dad needed to get it off is chest. That's what he told me, it may have gone down a bit like that. I wasn't there, so I don't know for sure. Dad's emergency stash of brown weed was now, "juss twigs wid seed". The pot was rare, even the Eastern District was dry. Not even any solids – apart from some shitty formula - no way Dad would sink so low and burn that. They'd both smoked off most of some dodgy hydro - because of the drought that's all Darren could get from his music school buddies - so were both primed to be suspecting.

Dad said, Darren's first comment after he told him about all the shenanigans with Vic was, "Sik man, wicked. Got any more pills?"

Darren was never one to miss an opportunity. Dad was kind of impressed with him. My father wondered out loud to me about those observing us, he thought it muss be higher than Old Bill.

He figured if man is scrutinising hard it muss be about Vic.

I nearly told him about Sam, but I juss couldn't do it.

I thought, why have some arsehole cuss-off Darren? Then tip us off? Perhaps it was psychological operations - stressing us out.

Or, maybe they juss fucked up.

Fucked up, and stressed out, speaking of Mum, she hadn't returned any of my calls. I tried to convince myself I didn't care.

I began to feel there was something iffy about the school after less than a month there. Even before Samantha asked me to sell out my people for a decent education, I had started to realise something was going on but I pushed it to the back of my mind. Sam's requests coupled with Dad's paranoia were the icing on the doughnut. The day after my visit to the church I decided to do a bit of investigation into my "new school."

Dad had started asking me a lot of questions about it but he hadn't quite tied it into his growing web of conspiracy else he probably would have sent me back to normal school.

The day after Dad mentioned the Solomon Islands, tried to convince me the house was bugged, I got to class and was told that Samantha had gone away - took off, burst, scarpered. Something personal had come up so she knocked me back on the Trust Fund. No big university, for now.

Gutted, I paced around and around couldn't concentrate at all. I juss wanted to see her again despite her attempts to buy me. I didn't tell Dad but later on at school that day, juss by "coincidence", the Solomon Islands got mentioned.

I was furious within, but from outside neither Rahiman nor Edwards seemed to notice. Despite having had Dad go on about them only a few hours before. I told them that I'd never heard of the Solomon Islands.

Maybe it was this kind of behaviour that had spooked BO Joe back when he tested me. I don't doubt that I had some problems, but these jokers weren't into helping me. They attempted to bribe me and were probably bugging my freaking home. I decide I'd had enough. Those that pretend to care, fuck 'em to smithereens - inconsistent jokers deserve what they get. I moved towards a war footing, gathered intel. I snooped around while acting as if working. I noticed a few things that would be useful later. The microwave in the upstairs kitchen might make a functional weapon, I tested that it worked. Then I declared home time and reached back to mine for the weekend.

Fi came back from school with her head hidden in a scarf. Crying she locked herself in the bathroom. Jan hit our yard about twenty minutes later. My sister screamed at me through the bathroom door that if I let him in she'd cut my bollocks off while I was sleeping. The way she said that I was sure I'd regret it if I disobeyed - and I was quite attached to my nutsack.

So I told her, "Ease up. He's not coming in if you don't say so."

I nearly got my head into the bathroom but she slammed the door shut again - oh shit. Fiona could be quite a handful if she lost her temper. She wouldn't back down. Skills can cut more than one way - the best part about you can be the worst. Most of the time she stayed out of trouble but when she got into situations it was because of not taking any nonsense, like the story that went into the family legend amplifier about ten months ago. It came out like this: as part of a project for teenagers likely to get up-the-duff way too early – she was given an infant simulator to look after. Looks juss like a sprog and you have to burp it; rock it; change its nappies; take care of it; stop its unbearable crying. A bunch of her spars took some of these robot-picney to Milton Keynes on a day trip run by some do-gooders.

She was walking along when a gang of local girls started to get brave – shout at them that they were slags; skets; sad breeders – treading foot on their turf. When one of this mob threw a can in the direction of her head Fiona pulled her fake tot from its pushchair – stepped to the ringleader. She took the baby by the leg, dashed its lifelike robot head straight into the teeth of the girl that was abusing her. Banged her, dropped her clean - K.O. The felled girl's terrified cronies ran off screaming as the baby started to cry.

The doll was resilient but not bombproof; it didn't survive what happened next. As the felled girl's crew spun off over tarmac Fiona took aim. She flung the child at them, a floppy boomerang. It struck one of the girls directly on the back of the bonce. Robot vs. human cranium, head to head - round two.

Unfortunately she chucked the replica child over a busy main road. The sight of a lifelike baby suddenly appearing in the air was quite a shock to some drivers - its face stained with the decked kid's blood; crying; cart wheeling over the carriageway; smacking a girl; then spinning off under some truck wheels.

It almost caused carnage.

It took Fiona a long time to live that one down.

I went and told Jan that he couldn't come in. There had been an eruption, my sister was having a freak out. Bless him; he looked really concerned for her. He seemed disappointed that she didn't want him in the house but he took it well. I told him to park arse on the steps for a while. I'd see if I could get to the bottom of it.

"Tell her, I'm raining too", he said.

I put my hand on his shoulder and said, "Safe".

Dashed on some music really loud for a while, it was Fi's sound track album to Kinky Boots, it was sort of a musical allegedly set in a half-arsed version of Northampton mixed up with Earl's Barton.

They'd made up a kind of mishmash of Abington Street, the Drapery and the Market Square in a warehouse somewhere, then stuck a fake version of the "Last People" statue in it. Wonder what they did with it when they'd finished with it. The film was supposed to be about the town because it was about shoes, as well as people here being bothered about a brother in a dress. I've seen plenty man in a dress walking around, no one gives a shit. Well okay, four or five trannies in the bus station and god knows what sex all the goths were at the top of Abington Street. It ain't Daventry, dragsters can walk around.

Well they can if they stay around the central sides. They don't make kinky boots here either they make them in fucking China like everything else.

The film was a feel fab fib and Sis loved it. So I cranked up choons and put the kettle on.

Fi came out of the bathroom during *I Want To Be Evil*. I saw she had a bruised eye. I was shocked but I didn't show it.

"Did Jan do that?" I joked.

She picked up a hairbrush, threw it at me. No; Jan wasn't the culprit.

"Well who did then?"

She juss started crying again. I put my arms around her, rocked her for a while as she sobbed.

After a few minutes I told her that I needed to go tell Jan that she was okay.

She grabbed my hand and said, "Don't tell him".

"Tell him what?"

"About my eye."

"Oh, that, so that's why you're crying," I teased her, "I thought the panda look was in." I thought I was being helpful. It had some impact. She hit me hard in the ribs, then half-smiled. She told me to tell Jan that she would call tomorrow. I told her he wouldn't care about a shiner, she could always cover it in some slap. But she wasn't so sure. So I went out - told him he'd better step; that my sister wasn't being slack, I'd get to the root of it he juss had to be patient. Go home - write her a letter and to make it musical. He nodded then chipped. I didn't know what she was playing at blanking her man, but obviously the eye wasn't fuckall to do with Jan. She had him under manners anyway. They'd been dealing for a while. May be it was a lover's ting, pointlessly making him fret coz she'd gone all screwface over what she looked like. Actually it was probably because at that point she couldn't face telling him the truth: he'd've got it out of her. But hey my sister can be pretty mysterious even to me, with my mega Ekman powers. Trying to figure out why other people do emotional shit is a waste of time. They most likely don't even know. If it had been true for me, why shouldn't it be true for everyone else?

I went back inside, said if she didn't tell me who did it I'd tell Dad that Jan had hit her. If she'd have stopped to think about it she'd have known I was lying. It wasn't very nice but I thought it might work. She told

76

me that she would pour water up my nose while I was sleeping - I would drown in bed. I laughed. After a while so did she. I took some ice from the top of the fridge, put it in a sock for her to press on her eye then gave her another hug.

I hung with Fi that night, and on the Saturday. I could tell that she was shook up. She didn't even look at her mobile.

Dad didn't say much juss, "You okay G'yal?"

She told him she'd walked into a wall. I don't think he bought it but like me he bit his lip. I borrowed Earl's brother's bike, went over to Kingsthorpe for fish and chips. I got her an eye patch from the chemists, after swiping some books about the brain from the Kingsthorpe library. I'd figured out how to mash the alarm system. I was shit hot. I told her that all the other girls were always pirating her look, kattin her hard. She was the scene-setter, so now the look was pirate. I said to her, "All dem girls will be wearing an eye patch."

She looked sceptical.

"I'll be your parrot," I said flapping my arms as I jumped in the air repeating over and over again, "Bugger off, Bugger off, Bugger off," in a high pitched voice. She flung a look at me, kissed her teeth, then started to laugh. She put on the eye patch, then spent fifteen minutes fannying around sticking some glistening shit to the front of it. It looked quite funky when she'd finished, on the black background she'd drawn a silver eye, in glitter.

I had talked her into leaving the house, juss as Jan stuck his letter through the door. This was followed by more floods of tears. Jan's skills were raw. Respect due. He'd written her THE LETTER, drawings - the works - took her twenty minutes to read it between sobs. This was followed by lots of rapid texting back and forth. Tings were nang, shabby, sik, gunay, grimey, wicked, excellent, top, ace, skill, peng, brilliant, triffic, tastic and cool. Well, they were a bit better. So it was mid afternoon before I managed to get Fi to leave the house. Jan had had to go off to some Polish event so couldn't come around till nex' evening. Being with Fi kind of reminded me of when I used to help Mum. For a little while I forgot all about vexing tings. I was close to my sister, which I hadn't really realised in a deep way before. She took my mind of all the shit that was going down. Someone had done violence to her defo. I could tell that from how she was reacting. I was going to get to the bottom of who but I decided to bide my time.

I was desperate to get out into town to show Fi my new toy.

Who hasn't looked at a cash machine wishing that it would start puking out dollars right at their feet non stop until it was rinsed? Hacking the tech was the most difficult physical mission I had ever turned my attention too, it had taken me the best part of three weeks. It was hard, fun though. Most of it I did in my head; that was the really taxing part. I liked finding new applications for commonplace items, that's the relaxing part.

The basis of the system was a mobile I'd extensively modified - added a few bits of my own. A bit of jiggery-pokery that I was very pleased with. I filled up her handbag with twennies till I had over two grand, then I juss walked away as corn continued to flow. When I got into Dychurch Lane I slowed down, caught some breath. I was acting a bit sketchy. Had a quick gecko about for unwanted man eyes or a robot gaze, removed the mask I was wearing then retrieved my jacket from where I had stashed it. I left the disguise on the ground behind the library. It was something Dad had had kicking round for years - a rubbery Thatcher. She didn't mean much to me. Dad couldn't even bring himself to say her name without turning all screwface. Still he had kept the mask for some reason, I don't think it was sexual. It smelt a bit iffy but it came in useful.

Fi was waiting in a café, one without CC-TV. I was charged. It had worked. I handed her the bag. She nearly shat herself with surprise, when she opened it. She slapped it shut again. I thought she would never stop giggling; saying, "Oh my God" over and over. Money can rent you some happiness. Funny, right then she forgot all about her eye. I could see it clear on her face I had changed her understanding of reality, transported her to a new world. The air smelt slightly of caramel. The autumn sun was setting outside. People drank their drinks all around. I was the calm centre of the Tornado. It was time to destroy our grey Kansas. With this toy we could repaint our lives buy a whole new canvas, whisk ourselves off to vibrant places at the click of a broken heel. I planned to empty masses of wall holes up in the Smoke. It would only be a matter of weeks before the banks figured out how to stop me. I'd need to move fast, create a few false idents - salt it away for a rainier day. Once I'd figured out a way to launder it: conseq' notes are a pain in the arse. Gold might be the way to go. Right then though, we went shopping.

Fi went into a kind of feeding frenzy. We splashed out on clothes, clothes, more clothes, lots of music, films, games, a few books, seven pairs of shoes, make-up, perfume, a stoosh watch for Jan, some food for Dad from Marks and Sparks. Then we went to Papa Chinos, sat down for some nosh and nyammed our faces. Never been in there before, it's the nuts. Then later in the phone-shop I dished out for a BlackBerry, so that I could contact Vic. Obviously I paid in cash, gave false details. Fiendish cryptography makes it the weapon of choice for any well organised criminal. I also got a rucksack which I filled with a load of camping supplies including a Maglite, plus a shed-load of *Midnight Runner* teabags. I was tea total, totally into tea - the only drug I was still mad for. *Midnight Runner* was so the best. It had a caffeine content equal to espresso. The sinister absinthe coloured Art Deco packet, with its warnings of heart attack, promised a *Naturally*

Increased Caffeine Experience - N.I.C.E. Very nice. It was the first one out, had started the whole craze for high-caff tea. It was still my favourite. We walked over from the market, grabbed a taxi back home from under the shadow of All Saints. Bloated sharks, the Hackney Carriage with its fish-eyed driver swam us through the traffic back to our port with the swag. He overcharged us but I didn't give a fuck. It was juss a little nibble in the wad, why quibble over a few quid? I still had over seven hundred nicker in notes. Fuck her Trust fund. There was plenty more where that came from.

Fi looked exhausted, but content. I knew tomorrow she would tell me the name.

In the end she told me without words. I juss saw it there iced on her face. It was Roger who'd hit her. Her Mum's latest flame. She told me that she was supposed to go over to see her Mum for Sunday dinner, but that she didn't feel up to it. I knew that some issues had been playing out, that's why she'd landed at ours but I hadn't realised that it was likely to be extending to the dishing out of beats to her swede. The jibber had given her a bloody shiner. There was a price. He had to pay it. If I told Dad he would go over there and launch him - ballistic. He could never cool down his temper over such matters. It was better that I sorted it. Suddenly I had a new enemy to place to the top of my list. Eye for an eye, well perhaps - but he was a muscle-bound fucker so I'd heard. Happy-slapping him would be a bit tricky. Justice should be more poetic, and I'm not Earl who would have a pop at manz for a wronglook.

I didn't want that kind of hassle.

After my punch up with the private security guards, I decided to keep fights to a distance, wherever possible. I had to protect my head; it was far too valuable to me. That's part of the reason I fried Tovey; dashing my noggin was a big no-no - a violation. I put my hand on her shoulder, told her I'd come with her, that we could get a cab. We had dosh now. She could test out her new clobber. I sort of suggested that she could pick up anything that she needed from there, hinting she'd never have to go back. She could style it out with me - avoid 'xtra agro. Never came out with it, or said it directly. I knew that if I made a big squeal about it, she'd never go over there. First shit first, I wanted to help her. If there was to be any revenge she'd need to enjoy it too. Well that was the plan then.

So together we reached to her Mum's sides. Fi didn't say much in the minicab. I told her we needn't stay long, get back quick then hang with Jan. I didn't like going east on any day. I knew we were getting close when we went past the Weston Favell Shopping shitehouse, a huge urinal of despair. It's the armpit of Northampton. It exists to make the bus station look nice in contrast. The driver made a point of telling us about all his on-board security. I felt like he was singling me out for the information. I didn't take it personally. At that point I wasn't entirely sure why I took the thermite with me; I thought it might be jokes.

Fi's Mum's house looked like the Bad Wolf could easily blow it down. I had a quick gander, stashed the thermite, then knocked on the door. Then a quick butcher's through the window. The folks were inside cotching in front of the TV with a few plates of cold food.

Dot - Fi's Mum - and Roger - Dot's bo - were very polite, civil. I could see that they were surprised, then slightly perturbed, to see me. Dot's eyes showed pleasure, then fear, like spotting a wasp on the edge of an éclair that you've taken a bite out of. Later still her eyes showed shame. Fi scarpered to her bedroom with her Mum, left me alone with the sad minger Roger who was concentrating hard on a porkpie. I chatted to him for a while took the measure of him. He was right up himself. The fuckhead seemed to have no feelings for others. The strongest emotion I detected in him was fear, probably of me plus Dad. I also picked up on his love for his enormous silver car, out of place in this neighbourhood - his big-man badge. Trust me he loved a machine almost as much as he loved his cock. Cocky that was him. I could see it clear, for real; the car was his only love separate from himself; the only thing he cared about. Other than those bits of his body that pleased him independently more than the whole of his carcass ever would. Humans were less important than his ride. The kind of seedy punter who spends too much time down the gym with semi-naked blokes, lots of mirrors, pumping away, gives it poonany this, pussyhole that, pum-pum the other. Always runnin down gyal - half the world's population were reduced, in what uttered from his cakehole, into rival gangs of bitches, slags, sketts, slappers, tarts, hookers, ho's, wastegirls and whores. They were *always* fighting for the opportunity to receive his seed - *always*. I could tell by juss looking at him that he was a predator. He didn't have much in the way of nice feelings. I do have a problem with some women, but at least I don't come on like that. No skills. It's not stylish. Keep your problems particular.

Roger gave it the reh, reh, reh; put the total cant in incantation. He tried to be creepy and he was; only not the creepy he wanted to be. He came on all Harry Potter, cloaks, tarot cards and auras: modern chicken's blood bizniz. Chanting on strong mystical gobbledegook - oooow, a scary man, he oozed a guzoo-guzum-guzumba-obeah-*psi*ance-darkness tip, his hoodoo voodoo doodoo trip. He called all his arse-talk, Magick; told me it was important to spell it with a K - apparently. It was pathetic really. He didn't even believe in it. He bored me. Ekman powers saw the charlatan clean. It was juss a tool in his manipulation kit. It had probably protected his car, to be fair.

He was cursed though, but I don't think he'd have the wherewithal to realise exactly what was missing in him. I faked interest in his magical achievements to see if I could nick some scam-man routines, but his badness was all very low-grade.

Halal the fucker in the bath then make black-magic-pudding out of his claret, that's what I felt like doing but it would involve getting too close to him. So I sat there nodding at his nonsense, while I picked at a sarnie, waiting for Fi to re-materialise.

Dad says that *on-the-in*, there's a pecking order: blaggers at the top, bacons at the bottom. Maybe Roger and I weren't so different. Who wants to be at the bottom of the pile? Perhaps I'm juss convincing myself that I'm better than him to justify what I did: I'm the baron, he's the nonce. Roger really wanted to feel *The Man* as somewhere deep in the abyss of him he didn't feel the man he wanted to feel at all. The best way he had figured out to achieve king monkey feelings, was to slap sistren about. Clearly a Fraggle, with a fickkle temper and a likkle fuse - red mist when pissed - usual story same old, same old. If I had thought to bring my flame-thrower with me I'd have barbied the bastard. Still, as it was, I had juss the right way to slap him down. He'd lucked out. It wouldn't be a long ting it would be quick, but we'd have to return to the vicinity later. I prefer to conjure flames in darkness. That was the plan then. We had to transport Fi's shit back home anyway.

Dot was under heavy manners. She wasn't how I remembered her from when I was a kid. She was a bit too particular in everything she did. Sort of like she'd been given a bit of freedom for my benefit, wasn't sure what to do with it. So was reverting back to trying to keep her fella happy by attempting to keep the place orderly, how he liked it. Roger had stamped his personality on the place pretty quickly. It was all too neat, carefully placed sorcery paraphernalia on a miniature shrine like Dungeons and Dragons bullshit. Dot needed to fix up and kick him out, cull the candles, kill the skulls - but it wasn't going to happen, her flame had snuffed out. Roger didn't have to follow Dot to keep her under control. He'd done a number on her. She'd do exactly what he said even if it meant driving her daughter away. A daughter, who the way Roger probably painted it to himself, was a rival for the attention of his cock. Power spun his prop. He'd have to get got.

Fi didn't say much to her mother when I was in earshot. I had the feeling that when Dot said, "Come back, whenever you want", that she was all knotted up about that prospect; wanting it, not wanting it - simultaneous. That's bad shit. She didn't come over too impressed with Fi's new threads. Like she found them threatening, maybe they reminded her of a loss. Or perhaps she sensed that Fi had blagged them somehow.

We carried the bags into the street. My new rucksack was already paying for itself. It was a good piece of kit. Good kit is where it's at. I wanted to wait outside for our cab. Dot's house was gently freaking me. It had much more space than ours but her yard felt claustrophobic. Nothing these people said was true - in a deep way - even where they put down their drinks was too controlled. I felt glad that Fi had Dad to be there for her, like he had been for me. He might be a bit slack, but you knew where you were with him. He had a heart. I told Fi square as we stood there that I knew for sure that it was Roger who'd hit her.

"It's hard sometimes to say shit, you don't think you'll be believed...You don't want to upset Dot..."

She nodded.

I told her straight that I thought it was clear that Roger was an arsehole, a woman hating scumbag, a control freak who was out for what he could get. It was a shame her mum couldn't see it, but that's love. My sister started to cry. She said faintly, "It was."

There would be ructions and repercussions. If she wanted we could sort him together, if she were up for it. We wouldn't involve Dad. Roger wouldn't have to know who his assailants were, we would do him as a team; not straight away though. When serving it cold the dish is improved by a dash of adrenaline added juss at the end, but not too much. She nodded softly. We would go home then we'd cook up the plan. Jan was supposed to be coming over so it would have to wait until he'd chipped. I thought that I needed to get a decent video camera first. Left my thermite where it was stashed. I was confident it would be there when it was needed as it juss looked like a lump of manky shit shoved in a hedge. On the way back we said very little. Fi stared out of the taxi's window. I could see despite everything she missed her Mum. Like me. It made me feel even closer to her. Maybe Roger was an apt stand in for my Mum's boyfriend; he was a suitable prick for me to kick against. Very likely I was really planning on attacking someone else through him. Well there was no fear that Mum's bag-head bo would ever have a striking silver car, that had all been booted away. Probably never gonna reach from Welwyn Garden City again, his only transportation running the beetle up the foil. A powder powered pedestrian - animal movements - he migrated with his monkey, chasing around his streets for a drag on the horse. It was deep autumn. There was a scent of fires and decay in the air. The cabbie was listening to orchestral music it had a sort of funeral feeling; death and taxis. The melody seemed to put me into a bit of a trance. I didn't notice at the time but I was absorbing that driver somehow.

We got back to ours juss in the nick. Tings had kicked off. Jan had Darren pinned to a wall in the street. One hand pressed decisively around Daz's throat, the other raised to strike him in the face. I chucked the cabbie too much dosh then bailed with baggage, Fi followed.

"Fuckin stop it now wingnut!" I shouted as I dropped the bags, marched towards him and gradually dropped my voice making it gentler.

"Come on Jan. I've resisted the urge t' dish it t' D for time. If I can, you can... Don't test me." Then I chuckled.

Something seemed to click, he lowered his hands sheepishly. Darren's eyes now looked too big for their sockets as he stared over at me, "Yush," he said, "Safe".

"You are now rudeboy", I smirked at him, "What did ya sell him?"

Fi marched right up into Jan's face, demanded, "Wahgowan?"

I suddenly felt sorry for Jan. I told them all to ease up; hush mouts. We didn't want to broadcast our bizniz to all-n-sundry. Daz said, "We gunnu be earwigged ya twat, if we chops inside man will be listening for real. Ayyerd?"

He started blubbering on about some sort of conspiracy stuff. I told him it was okay. We'll all take a pootle to the Nenn, no one was to say nuttin until they'd calmed down first. No back chat - end of. Everyone was to stay shtumm or I'd turn screwface. Go malevolent on the posse. Dish out licks - simple as. I was bossing my spars about a bit but I thought it was for the best, let the epinephrine tide subside; get rational. The stolen brain-chem book I'd been reading was very useful but there was nothing in it which even hinted at what could have happened to my cortex.

We would chat on at the river one at a time and no shouting. They looked tired all of them. They nodded then gave me a hand getting Fi's shit inside. As I grasped my backpack, I looked up. In the air above the estate there were three or four miniature planes. Tiny drones hovering, I wondered what they were for.

The aircraft didn't seem to follow us, they juss hung over the estate. We walked for about a quarter of an hour, didn't stop until we'd reached a small waterfall - plenty of fizzy noise to allay Darren's fear of the electronic ear. I think he appreciated it. The walk and the water were calming. D didn't even moan about being near what he called, "nature". It transpired some anonymous caller had tipped off Jan's parents about Fi. Told them Jan had been spending time hanging at a known criminal's yard with a young girl. Bad timing, Darren had been jokingly threatening to blackmail Jan a couple of nights before - one of his wind-ups. Darren looked smaller not his usual puffed up self - remorseful. He denied doing the deed but felt he'd given the listening beast the idea. He didn't hold grievances against Jan. He said he'd been correct in trying to beat him. That was a bit harsh. Darren had more soul than he normally let on, or perhaps he'd been at the shrooms. I knew Daz was telling it straight. So did everybody else. Jan took in Darren's side then said he was sorry; stuck his chin up and his hand out, shook Darren's paw. One of the blokeiest things I've ever seen Jan do, other than trying to strangle D that is.

If Daz didn't make the call then Jan had no issues. No beef. But who was fucking with them, and why? I had some ideas about that, so did Darren. I thought it best if I kept talk of them to a minimum. If we went too into it then I'd have to tell them all about the pill, it seemed to me that it might put them in danger. I thought it best not to freak Fi out anymore. So I told them that Darren might be right someone could be buggin ours because of a piece of Dad's folly, but it was unlikely. I winked at Darren. I told them all that it didn't mean that these mysterious listeners dashed in Jan to his folks. That it could have been anyone who saw the love birds together, with no motive other than spite.

It was reasonable, possibly convincing; Fiona's pissed a few people off in her time. Jan though, he didn't really have any enemies. Despite what I said, I thought it was nameless beast doing it. Psychological operations, increasing the pressure, trying to break us up - get to Vic. I was reading it all through my war goggles.

Jan could always sense when I was twisting.

"How did they get my number?"

"Could be man at the Polish school for all I know."

I told them that the best they could do was to try to rescue what they could from the situation. Then see what occurs.

I suggested a strategy for sorting his parents: that Fi should go with him to meet them. Dished out a pile of dunzi so they could go out for a meal, or get a take away first. Basically the plan was to go to Jan's yard together; be nice, be caring, but be firm. Love is the most important ting. Parents are coming on strong, because they're concerned for Jan, are worried about him. Use it against them. Tell them straight that if they don't stop poking their noses in, never try to control their dealing again, let both of them get on with it; then they will walk into the nearest cop-shop dob themselves in for sex crimes. They would put each other on the kiddie-fiddlers register, and it wasn't a list of young musicians. That would fuck each other's lives up good and proper - shame to the family, all that nonsense. Actually I didn't know if they were dealing with each other; whether he'd got with her. Not for sure, I hadn't actually caught them grinding.

What I did know was that they cared for each other a lot. I could see that in their faces surer than anything. Whatever they were up to they would be careful, respectful. Strong religious types are obsessed with screwing down fucking, fucking up shagging. So it probably wouldn't be good enough for Jan's Mum. She'd juss have to put up with it - get used to it in the end.

His Mum was a bit of a nightmare but alright really. Her heart was true. She wanted the best for Jan. She should have realised that saying no to lovers is the worst kind of action. It's not as if it's not the basis of a huge amount of stories full of death, destruction and mayhem or ting. Pragmatic blackmail seemed like the quickest way to chill his folks out.

I'm sure they'd find it very chilling.

Jan nodded and said, "They won't like it, but it might work. They know I do what I say I'm going to do. I suppose if it doesn't, I can always tell them that Fi's pregnant".

I laughed.

Poor Jan, at least I had Dad he'd never come on like that. Jan's folks were the traditional happy family proper, Dad and Mum together since day one. Through his folk's eyes I only had a Dud and a Mad.

During all of this Fi was silent. She seemed to have forgotten totally about her eye.

She was even more practical, than me. What she said was, "I suppose it's worth a go babe, Gran will let you stay with her anyway. 'Charmin young man', she calls you."

She stroked Jan's face. Granpa and Gran first sparked their romance when she was even younger than Fi, so she wasn't likely to get all 'xtra over it. Darren started playing out music over his mobile. I guess he'd made this nature scene long enough. The lovers headed off to confront the demon of religion in its human manifestation, Catholic parents. I guessed it would bring it to a head, whatever.

We walked back towards the estate, Darren and me. Drones still hung over it. Darren continued to nice up the area, playing out some choons. He didn't seem to notice the aircraft, he was lost in music, thin and baseless though it was - like most of his plans.

I thanked Darren for not mentioning the pill. He said that he'd told Dad he'd hold it down.

"I wen dain Marvin's rudi. He was diggin in his crates, he found summut." He handed me a Marmite Jar. I opened it. It looked like it was half-full of yeast extract like you'd expect. "Hash oil," he said, "does the trick. Two hundred notes. Pass it t' the old-man."

Dad would be toasting, for sure.

I wanted to bring my plans forward, go to London as soon as I could - start robbing cash machines. I was running out of time. Perhaps go up for few days, get a hotel. It was all going to blow, it was inevitable. My teachers and the military had as good as declared war on me - sell out my family? Me? If they'd really been fucking with Darren and Jan then they'd fired the first salvos too. It didn't matter, I planned my assault; first strike or counter attack, I didn't give a fuck what it was. I would dash them with pyrotechnic exquisiteness - sun-face, lick all dem man. Plasma, the fourth state - they'd catcha fire.

Even then I oscillated between cold rage, and longing for Sam. My pining didn't last. If anything once it had passed; when I'd returned to my screwface attitude the vexation was deeper, colder.

I doubted Jan's folks were the sort to exorcize him, or blast him with shotgun. Black-eyeliner was one ting, but could they handle Fi in the Flesh?

I went home. The yard was silent. Dad was sitting in his chair staring into a space that wasn't there. He was enduring one of his deflated days: nah man no bloodclaart ting dem. No curtains open; no music on; no beer chilling; no tea brewing; no food cooking; no energy; no chances; no good; no example; no life; no lover.

No weed.

No.

Dad had swept the floor, left the dustpan on the table. That's how I knew he had neesh; trying to herd up a few isolated particles, a moping herbsman looking for long lost blimbs, green crumbs of his girlfriend to put a fire to.

"From Darren," I said as I flung him the Marmite jar, "your mate."

Dad got busy constructing. I went and crashed out. I was suddenly knackered, it was only juss the evening but I needed to kip. Only meant to have a snooze, fell asleep in my clothes; slept for fourteen hours - clean.

Head on the pillow full of formulas, dancing wiring patterns, bright numbers floating in electric grids in front of me. They seemed have personalities, started speaking to me. Muss have lost consciousness, suddenly I was in the clear night sky flying over my house chill wind in my face. Hands stuck out above my head like superman. I was dreaming but I knew it. Felt it like it was real, unlike anything that had ever happened to me before. This was not your normal kind of dream nonsense, this was something else. A new state of mind different from being awake, different from dreaming. I was filled with a sense of elation. I had no idea that such a brain condition was possible. I smelt the sting of ice air; saw spit fly out of my mouth towards the ultra bright stars; saw steam breath freeze; heard my voice laughing manically as I looped the loop. All of it totally real, vivid, concrete - I knew I was fast asleep on my bed but this was like being awake, only better. And later I remembered it all like it had happened for real. Not a half recalled rapidly fading dream ember, but a normal everyday memory. Below me on the road a taxi pulled up, flashed its headlights in the darkness. I hovered above the car; cleared my throat; gobbed - bull's-eye. I flew down landed gently by the cab. It was the same one that took us back from Fi's parents.

The driver from the trip back from Fi's got out of the car. He stood on the path. Only now he was wearing a panto costume like from The Forty Thieves.

He said, "Get in. You're driving."

Got into the cab was juss about to close the door when the cab driver climbed in using the same door. At first it felt like he had sat on my lap, the weight of him sitting on top of me; his smell like fish, chips and fags. He began to melt into my body. I absorbed him. The strangest feeling, a bit like submerging into water - only it tickled.

Then there was only me in the car. I saw myself in the mirror, now dressed like Ali Baba. I began to drive. Drove all night all over my dream town; had never driven a car before, but seemed to know how to drive - in dreamland anyway. Hours of practise on Gran Turismo and Forza Motorsport probably helped. As the sun started to come up I swung the car back in to our road, parked like a professional, got out of the car - woke up. Lay on top of my bed still in my clothes, no costume. The sun was indeed coming up, went to the window to check but there was no taxi there. Didn't really think there would be but the experience felt so real, I had to look. I decide first opportunity I got I should test to see if these luminous night skills were carried over into the everyday grey world. I would find out if I could drive in waking reality.

Dad was up, drinking tea, watching the morning news hysteria; as usual some pampered clone was trying to make us crap brown-piss, while my old man munched nyamming like a mindless machine on a crumpet that dripped red jam.

Today's tasty terror, pure agro; the diabolical shenanigans of disgraceful yoot: playing out; running beyond boundaries; thinking they're making their own mistakes. They'd done the dance. A percussive soundtrack pounded my head and forced me along. I watched a rapid hotchpotch of shots, extensive examples, evidence of all sorts of larking about after dark. Plenty naughtiness in freeze dried fragments of footage, selected highlights of low-life to stab a middle finger into the eyes of the muddle aged. This country's ever present cameras beamed right at me in the centre of England. I don't blame this influence for making me sprint amok but they certainly set me up for the day. And what a day it was.

Strictly it was programming, pure programming, likely to invite and incite more of the same rather than get to the roots. Monkey-see-monkey doss, definitely bro. Hey kids have a swig, neck a bit of this before you go to school. Taste what young-uns do when the anointed supervisors aren't around. It puts face on TV. Join in. Join the tribes, initiate.

Misbehaviour, futile, the way to grow: only kind of freedom for all ah we. Never going to amount to a fuck anyway - outclassed - stay where you are in one kind of prison or another. Our TV realm it's a closed circuit. It's not interested in you, unless you bring some really big noise. That's what I found out.

Come! Witness! There they all were constant nuisances; joy riders; ram raiders; fire makers; racist oxygen-wasters; stealers and thieves of all kinds; griftters, grafters, graffers; taggers; tuggers; waggers; bullies; vandals; street-gangsters; haters; skaters; baiters; dog fighters and drug takers - an onscreen tornado. Performances of badness perpetrated by school age scallywags - fickle gyals and likkle bwoys - feral adolescents from around our kingdom. This nation has talent, more and more everyday; swearing gits; wankered wingnuts; masters of slackness, their booze fuelled dossing jolting my morning eyes. The box, boxing me upside the head, see it deh - on our TV like a stupidness Oscars.

Knocking down ginger wine; taking cherry's in doorways; attacking hoaxed-out firemen, shooting them up with pyrotechnics, flinging dirty pins at their bright engine, needling them to turn on their hoses.

Larger-boys larging it in alleyways; banging and stomping at random, having a jolly.

The tide of violence continued to wash over me. Havoc at the beach - sticks, rocks and blood - holidaymaker hooligans vs. seaside hoodlums. Zoom in on a zoot, in the lips of one dreadlocked yoot sitting quite peaceful, suddenly surrounded by snarling police dogs.

Spiteful gobby robbing hoodies spitting, running down main streets; steaming and taxing, taking all they can. An odd food fiend looking to get lean gets an unexpected hit by crashing a car stolen juss two minutes before.

Paraded; an entire estate of 'erberts who'd been running with rocks and powder, now all in cuffs somewhere in the Smoke.

Pixelated mugs of muggers, merchants of menace moving to you having your mobile - tucking you in - bruking ya up an' feeling no way.

Infrared chopper shots hallucinogenic and predatory - vexed beast in progress, eagerly running down persons unknown.

Unruly puppies aggravate the whirlybird and scatter.

Pig eyes dazzled and dazed by laser pointers swiped from a Tesco - the flying swine got quite pissed off.

Then nex' man running from sirens, he's not going out like that; street running freestyle! See him escaping down a manhole, majestically shown in super slo-mo. Mobs of cheeky sods and surly yobs, nippers and NEETS of both sexes on public transport flossing, showing off for their phone-cams - giving it all the reh, reh, reh. Goading, prodding, cussing - concealing fear in accusing sneers. Don't eye them they're all looking to bounce you, tetchy hands gripping on household blades. See the hustlers and hasslers that are attempting to drop man, giddy on violence they look for beef. Going commando style others clap you down, buss a gun on you, ben-'up your head.

I went and got a cup of tea and thought about what I'd been watching. Who is it that benefits most from this kind of news-vert? Do news bulletins need pounding background music? Maybe Dad was right when he'd say that the filth and courts have an interest in keeping a ready amount of criminals about. The ones that grab the yoot, snap them, develop their tendencies, expose them to jail chemistry, fix the gangsta identity like an old style photograph and make sure we have a new generation to keep them busy till pension time. Play right into their hands. It probably went deeper than that. Still there's no better way to have an excuse to control people, than to encourage them to be misbehaved. Naughty is always what you get when you make a boredom farm and there are plenty of those.

The kettle rumbled slightly and a piece of bread popped up out of the toaster. Those electric jobs probably kill more citizens than criminals do. People are always sticking metal shit into them, and they're plugged right in to the main line. It might be a good idea to design a totally safe toaster and shit-up the nation into buying it; like they're scared into buying everything else. Little angelic kids gripping sizzling forks while burning up in heavenly blue flames their hair standing to attention as their eyes fry in their skulls like two small eggs. That would make a good ad campaign. Perhaps I should have set Darren up with that idea. He'd have probably made a go of it.

I took my hi-caf tea back into the room with Dad. He was still watching the discussion about the teenage apocalypse.

The true top-tops are the ones with plans t' learnya the hard way, as a voiceover on that video stream made clear. Someone high up the food chain pontificated and pronounced, smaller government and more jails - apparently. How'd they manage to work that out? A politician's mouth is a disgusting place. To keep the illusion of running tings they'll do it all, whatever - deceitful. They make us feel like parasites, when it's our blood they spill and sup. And they know we know. It's blatant. Dem vampires call us the stakeholders. They're scared of us; they want everyone else to be too. Separate and triumph, always a useful strategy.

They call me a terrorist. I don't bizniz. That's the script they boiled me down to. Even when you kick off a spectacular rampage, buss a move so tasty it's wittered about earth-wide, people don't really want man three dimensional. News-report soup is thin, processed, gives us the shits; contains mainly spicy bits of rabbit, nothing that can sustain the brain. They eat you for breakfast, puke you up all watered down for an audience to feed on too - juicy. Then forget you. Flick onto any news channel; gawp at the media gobbing on about itself attention span rotting before the eyes, repeating itself over, over, faster, faster - drooling like a sniffed-up toe-rag, tooting their own horny horn, never quite spurting out the actual end of the world.

It neutralises the sense in people.

Dad was in oblong-eyed flat-screen oblivion, captivated by the latest recreational revelations. He faffed about with his two-lighter system trying to get a flame; one lighter had flint, the other had gas, but the magic wasn't working between them. Dad kissed his teeth.

Then muttered to himself, "Weh de blood fy-yah ah g'wan? Chu!"

Finally he got combustion, smiled, and re-lit his butt.

"More fire rasta. More fire."

I asked him, "Where Fi at?"

He said, "Wha?"

The spell bust, he turned his eyes to me. He told me that she didn't come back last night, stayed over at Gran's.

I tried to call her up but her mobile wasn't on, neither was Jan's. I left Dad at the camp started to tread foot towards school. I was late, didn't give a toss. Tried Fi again, still nada. I worried about her.

Bloody clouds were clotting together in the west a warning for government shepherds. Sunlight had fully ripped back night's skin, new day flesh raw and red on the human sky; delicious late autumn morning, good for a rampage, or summut.

I noticed that there was still a drone hovering over the estate catching the early light it shone in the east, a tiny star of Bethlehem, heralding re-birth. I walked towards the river chewing on my grievances.

A quarter of an hour later I sauntered down the school driveway. Right before me was Samantha. She was emerging from the smoky glass of a shiny black Jaguar XF. She clocked me, slammed the door, tried to look apologetic.

"School's shut today. I should have rung you."

I realised all of a sudden that she was afraid, scared of me. My Ekman powers saw it clean. She reached quickly for a spray in her handbag, showered herself in atomised particles of deception. She smiled in my direction, a charm offensive. She looked exhausted. I walked towards her feeling like I should kick off - give her a taste of my opinion. I grinned. Found myself asking her to let me sit at the wheel of her car. She said it was a friend's, that she'd borrowed it. I could tell that she was lying about it for some reason. I told her I wanted to show her something, and I did. It was time to see if I could live the dream; the perfect opportunity to experiment. I opened up the driver's side, got in, shut the door. She got into the vehicle, in the front next to me, closed her door. Then I asked her for the key. I told her I needed to play her something on the stereo. She said it didn't need one it was a keyless ignition her presence in the car would make it work. She handed the dongle to me. I inspected the special fob that made the ignition work, and then dropped it at my feet.

"juss wanna try something" I told her, "Never driven a real car before, did you know that?"

I rapidly stuck it in gear, exploded off up the drive then out onto the Welford Road at increasing speed, changing up through the gears like I'd done it for years. Samantha screamed at me.

"Stop! Stop you idiot – Stop it now!"

In the few seconds that it took her to get her door open we were already going far too fast for her to jump, nearly fifty miles an hour and rising rapidly. She shut the door again. She obviously realised that it would be dangerous for her to grab at me. She reached for her seatbelt, put it on. Then she sat frozen in the luxury leather her eyes scanning the road and the mirror. Agitated, her left hand was pulling at her green hair. She didn't seem to be that surprised that I'd suddenly learned to drive. Her mind was clearly on self preservation.

So this is why the boy-racers teefed cars. I could see the attraction. Adrenaline brightens everything and everything is in the moment. Felt my heart machinegun, but I didn't crash. I drove like I'd been rally driving all my life. I was sucked into it like when I used to play Gran Turismo for days. It was like my dream. I loved it. We headed north speeding down the hill out of town towards the Brampton villages merging more and more with the machine. Samantha tried a different approach, tried to talk rationally to me asked me what was wrong? She came over all sympathy, trying to twist me.

"What's got into you? You know I like you - let's just stop the car shall we? And talk reasonably."

I told her to shut up, hush 'er mout'. We were past all that. Instructed her to put some music on the stereo or I would deliberately crash the car going as fast as it could go. Did she want to find out how good the airbags were? I wanted her to tell me how this was possible, how could I have learnt to drive like this in one night while I was asleep? I knew that she worked for the military. I wanted to know what they knew about me. If she wanted to explain it to me then I would listen. Otherwise I would keep driving much too fast for the road conditions, maybe we would both be transformed into a squished-up can of corned-beef leaking on a roadside oak. That would bring things to a head. Headlong into headlights, head into heels, head-on into the headlines, young hedonists going out together, finally; like the dead Princess and her pissed-up driver.

"How should I know?" she pleaded.

The music she selected was some sort of folk choral piece I'd never heard before; women singing on mass, perhaps from Eastern Europe somewhere. Maybe it helped me to loosen up. It was like I was sitting beside myself, super calm, super vex - simultaneous. Everything went rollercoaster. I almost rammed several other vehicles off the meandering country road; suicidal overtaking, reckless - as swift as I could - we burned along.

Not too foolishly though, didn't really fancy being brown-bread toast.

This went on for about five minutes with Sam looking more and more twitchy. She said nothing until she blurted out, "Look you're, well you're, and well you're very special. Gifted even. I am… impressed…You should stop now."

I began to feel kinder towards Sam. Maybe it was the pathetically stifled sound of terror in her words or the way she tried to come over all authoritative with her middle class tones, or simple flattery from a fit woman; or perhaps whatever she had sprayed on herself began to work its magic. Possibly it was the novelty of the excitement, the feeling of being in control behind the wheel. I suppose abuse of power should come as no surprise, to anyone. It's the whole point of authority isn't it? Maybe I was on a dominance trip. Samantha was starting to give me the horn again. It was a familiar pattern of thought my mind slipped easily back into it. I'd rehearsed many a saucy scenario in my mind's eye since I'd met her. I checked myself out in the mirror to make sure I was looking my best. I wasn't. I really should have lost the bum-fluff, but otherwise I was okay. One other good side to that blue pill was I never had spots again. Zippo zits since I split from the sleeping-bag chrysalis and re-emerged. It was almost worth going through juss for that. It's the acme of anti acne.

Like the countless times I'd wanted her before. Those gooey repetitive fantasies and feelings they'd clicked back in with the excitement of the drive; began to consume me, pulling me into the same old fleshy clockwork of tension and release. Sticky situation - I was juss about to cross the border into clear foolishness and deep folly, pull over to try and cop off with her, when she messed it up by speaking.

"I'm sorry about the other day."

Punching my erotic feelings where it hurt. It all rushed back: the church, her lies, images and emotions from outside St Mary the Virgin, her absence, the bugging, the offer to sell out Vic. It all conspired to pour arctic slush on my love blaze.

I was seriously conflicted, then it passed.

We were mismatched unattached disconnected. I was off the hook. I no longer engaged with her. For a moment I felt like puking the sense of loss was so strong. Then I noticed her eyes were now a different colour. They were hazel. She muss have been wearing some kind of contacts during her previous meetings with me. Then my mind seemed to click back on. Yeah.

I thought perhaps I should secure Sam so she couldn't escape, take her to the church and destroy the building right there in front of her - kibosh the temple to lies. I didn't take long to change my mind. Chicks in peril are dull blud, too much damsel in distress shit in the world. Seen masses of movies and games with some whimpering bird rescued by the big I-am from the monster man. No surprise I should have some of that action movie shit in me, but only a tad. It gets boring very quickly.

That wasn't the kind of psycho nut-job role I had in mind for myself anyway. Prefer movies with strong women. Sam was a bit of a disappointment.

I told Sam to throw her mobile out of the window. Then a few miles on I would pull over, let her out. She hit the window control, reached into her bag, did as I asked; probably as she'd been trained to do. She tried to reason with me, I juss turned the music up louder. There was nothing more to say. It was time to separate. Divorced from reality, I might have been but leaving Sam abandoned at the roadside in the middle of Northamptonshire wasn't even half-way to revenge city. I'd turned cold inside, time to turn on the heat. The authorities had rejected me, I cast them off. It was their loss. No fear that I would ever voluntarily go back with them again. I would jealously guard my freedom. It was time to split, to join with Vic.

I left Samantha walking somewhere out on the road beyond Ravensthorpe - towards the motorway at Crick. Drove off sensibly - heading back towards town. I didn't want her to be injured by what I'd decided to do next, but I didn't want to see her again. I tried to feel older. Hoping somehow that might stop me coming to the attention of any beast on wheels that might be in my vicinity. The slightly tinted-windows were lucky for me. I only caught site of one bully-van, but nothing happened. I drove on. If I could learn to drive, by juss watching someone, absorbing them, I wondered what other skills I might be able to arm myself with in dreamland.

Yes blud, I was energized.

Sam got smaller in my mirror as she stood alone under a leafless tree. I felt a twinge of sadness. It was over. At least I got to dump her.

My rampage had kicked off.

Fi sent me a text saying that she was okay but would be busy all day as she was helping Jan clear the spare room at Gran's. It didn't go too well with the parents, they'd flung Jan out. Having thought it through I decided it was better that I didn't involve her directly in my developing plans. There was no point in giving *The Power* the opportunity to lock my sister up. I'd originally wanted to work together with Fi on sorting out her Mum's bo; planned to avoid the blokey heroics formula, but it was not to be. I had to do him on my own. Still sort of sad about that. At least I'd get it on video for her.

I drove up to the school. No other cars outside. I ditched the wheels then bailed. I followed the procedure that Dad had explained to me. I sent a text using the new BlackBerry with the code phrase: ". . .*to the people no delay*" Then I waited.

5 seconds later I got a reply.

"OS MAP 152: 802513: Salcey: 23:00. Cause distractions. Destroy sim-card. Disconnect phone battery."

I was up for it.

The door to the school was easy to kick open. I took a shifty shuffty around, no one in there. I found a copy of the right Ordnance Survey map in the library area. I'd used it in a project a couple of weeks before. No documents relating to me though, none in the car either - shame. Classified that's what I am, that's what we all are; defined, confined, constrained.

I went upstairs to the kitchen area. Impulsively I scrunched up a few pages of some mindless tabloid newspaper that was abandoned half-read on the table, stuck my sim-card inside the screwed up paper, wrapped up the chip. Picked up a box of matches from next to the cooker, set the news a fire. Batter the place. Then I put the blazing lump of codswallop inside the microwave with relish, turned it on max, set for an hour. I wanted to generate my own plasma screen: the energy of a star, the fourth state of matter transforming The Sun newspaper. It seemed somehow apt. I saw the flame transform, then the pulsing plasma dance above a plate full of headlines and tits. Interesting fumes seeped out from the metal box – chemical smoky-reeking smog of war. The microwave hummed like a substation. Dancing energy, that's what the universe is and it can be liberated. On the other side of the room at the cooker I turned on the gas on the hobs, but I didn't light them. I listened to how that lovely gassy hiss made a discordant harmony with the grinding electric hum crackle. Then I legged it - chipped rapido. Goodbye to my school daze.

The eventual explosion wasn't massive, but I heard it over the sound of the river and the fire alarm as I made my way back to Dad's. I should have done her poxy car an' all, it's what Darren would have done. Balls.

A dark fist of smoke filled the sky behind me as I walked back to the yard. I began to hear two-tone sirens. It is a feature of rampages that they're not very environmentally friendly, it's the only part of the carnage that I feel stink about. That and later - when I split from the betting shop - I turned back to admire my handy work and saw the face of Sue, a friend of my Mum's from way back, she was lying on the ground in the street surrounded by smoke. She fought her body for breath. The asthma snakes coiling round her lungs fed on panic. I'd made that happen to her. It didn't feel very good. I turned away and called her an ambulance on my old mobile, and didn't look back.

After torching the school I openly walked back to our house to get my supplies. I'm sure I was watched by the remaining drone. I didn't care. I think it was waiting for Vic to show. I was still bait.

I intended to figure out how to hack-jack one of those remote-controlled spy planes at some point. It struck me that there's a weakness in having un-staffed equipment. Vulnerable to remote interference: I'll be jammin'.

I thought perhaps once I'd seized one I could fit some kind of weapon system to it. That might be fun.

I saw Dad. He signalled for me to follow him outside. I didn't give a bugger for the bugging devices, but I went along with the old sod. I told him I was off to meet Vic. It might get tricky, he might wanna stash his tings. I'd juss burnt down the school.

Dad looked solemn. He embraced me. Said, "Damn! T'rahtid. Back in da day I-an-I wanted t'do dat, ya know?"

Dad sort of tried to smile but looked pained. "Deep aggravations check I, for real. Sufferations."

I looked him in the eyes, we both tried to fight back tears.

Dad knew I had to leg it. He shook his head and said, "Tings agwan. Tings agwan."

He left me and went inside, then came back.

My Dad, ever the herbsman, handed me a small parcel of tinfoil which I opened. It wasn't his usual betting slip wrapped parcel. It contained half of a blue pill. He told me he'd only spiked me with part of it, as I was a yoot. He muss have figured the brain expander worked like an aspirin, or summut.

I examined the remaining half of the pill, "Is it ital?" I asked him.

Dad laughed.

"So take it." I pushed it back towards him.

"Nah man dem ting deh, obeah business - pure. Me cyaan tek it."

I remembered my plan from when I was first spiked, to drug Dad right back. That would have to wait. I got my shit together, hugged Dad strong and long.

"Tell Vic - sorry."

I nodded and told him that I would.

The pill had been meant for Dad who was hesitant to turn himself into a brainiac. I wonder what Vic would say when he found out Dad tested it out on me.

On toes I jogged through the estate hooked up with Darren juss outside the bookies. All my stuff in the new rucksack on my back. The turf accountant was where Darren's Dad usually was to be found. Darren had juss been checking him. A group of the usual personalities had gathered outside in a circle. I walked over to it. Then took off my bag; panted for breath. Darren looked over to me. On the floor at his feet was Norman.

Someone had cut the power, he wasn't electric anymore. He was dead. A small amount of blood came out of his ears. There was the smell of shit.

The location of the body outside the shop showed he had died defying his ASBO. There was further evidence of the breach: a small pool of piss against the betting shop front. Norman frozen staring up into the sky still held his cock in his hand; caught short; forever taking the P; pissed his life against the wall. The understanding Norman's soul was underway, suffered the final sundown. No more underpaid underclass underdog underworld for him, no rehab now to undergo. This neglected dreamer was looking forever beyond the breadline frontline. His dead gaze penetrating through the bullet-proof-glass ceiling that's so low here that you can reach up and touch it. A bottle of Fortisip and can of Tennant's Super at his feet seemed like an improvised tribute, perhaps they'd be placed here in piles like bouquets of flowers for the pharaoh of booze, on that everlasting bender in the sky.

Darren said that Norm had cried out, "Mum!" then had fallen backwards, smacked his head on the concrete, never moved again.

Hot tears blobbed my vision. I knelt down next to him. Stroked his head, closed his eyes. I took his knob, stuck it back in his trousers and zipped him up.

"Eeeeee nasti! Necro batty-man tramp lover!" said Darren, with all the insight and sympathy that he was known for. From a chap who was happy to accompany me in attempting to dig up the body of a dead Princess. In fairness to him, he was trying to make me laugh. It was the shock.

I gave him the look – and he fell silent.

This man, Norman, was supposed to be one of the ones breaking up our so called society with his bad-minded behaviour, an anti-social – like me – unwanted. He might have been at the bottom of the pecking order, but he was our society as far as I could see. He'd done a lot more good and lot less harm than some pussyclaart banker; wanker lawmaker or tight-fisted pawnbroker.

The only life that was cheap to Norman was specifically his. He would never have sent humans off to die for no reason overseas; spied on his own; killed benefits; issued ASBOs.

He would quote bits of pissed poetry to me. His favourite, "For every thing that lives is holy, life delights in life." He was better than those pricks who claim to be in charge of us – and he was a total mess. Despite his problems the man burst with good tings, his final action a protest.

I heard sirens closing, time to skedaddle. I stood up shouldered my bag walked slowly away, Darren following behind me. I added the betting shop to my list as a tribute. Torch the fuckin' place and done, simple as. A vodka Molotov - that would be the way. Laws don't stop anyone from doing sod-all they're used to try and punish you *if* you get caught.

I decide to link up with Earl before I chipped. So what if I wasn't allowed round there. Screw the ASBO. I wanted to borrow a bottle of spirits and I'd left my flamethrower with his brother. I figured I owed my friend an apology for the bizniz with the Princess, and I was abandoning him too.

As soon as we got to Earl's Darren insisted that I, "Wash those manky smeggy hands now bruv!"

I did as he said, laughing. He could be a dildo but he tickled my funny bone. If it was up to Darren the whole world would be sprayed with disinfectant, regular - daily.

In the few weeks since I'd last seen Earl he had grown noticeably. He was transforming into a beast of muscle. He'd been hanging with some Christian weightlifters that pushed metal for God. The peer pressure cooker of his new group seemed to have rapidly steamed his head which was now full of notions of salvation, sin, and the picking up of immensely heavy stuff on a regular basis. He reckoned the key to life was to take the weight of the world, and then to transform it.

"So you're not doing steroids?" I asked him.

"Nah man."

"You reckon Jesus was a weightlifter?"

"Musssss Beeelieve!"

But I didn't believe.

"Truss me, our Lord carried da cross 'ndat. KnowhatImean blud? Overstan' me?"

"A shirt-lifter moi-ol'-boody – never a weightlifter – Jesus was gay f'sure. Most priests are, f'real." Darren joined in the theological discussion.

"Leave it!" I told D – but Earl was laughing.

"It's all good." Earl nodded positively at me then pointed at Daren. "It's all good my bredren. Tell dat bwoy deh - God loves chi-chi man too."

Something had defo changed with Earl, it wasn't juss his increasingly muscular body. Peace and love directed at homosexuals, was not what I expected to hear from him. From the look on Darren's face, neither did he; his attempted wind-up had sprung right back on him. He wasn't having much luck in the leg-pull department lately.

Norman had no one, spent much of his life on the streets. I made Earl swear-down – promise to Jesus, and on the life of his Playstation, that he would help sort out a funeral for him. His weight pumping pals would assist with sending him off. They'd probably enjoy carrying the casket. I bunged him all the notes I had left. Darren could probably have done it, but he'd have put too much effort into figuring out how to skank anyone who turned up. Increased the turnout by having a mega prize raffle draw at the crem', sold hot dog sausages in little bread coffins.

I was surprised at what had happened with Earl in so short a time. People can change, and fuck knows I know that. It seems that faith in God can have a power akin to military drugs.

Change happens all the time anyway, sometimes it's a good ting - but not in the case of Mum.

I tried calling her from Earl's juss before I left. No response. I wanted to fling my old mobile away but I needed it for later.

Darren and I left Earl bench-pressing.

We walked for about half-an-hour. No sign that we were followed. The drone held position in the increasingly grey sky. We walked until we could no longer see it, then I decided to get Darren to show me how to hot-wire a car.

His twocing career finally came in useful, robbed a four-by-four from Kingsthorpe village. He was freaked to see that I could handle the truck so well, wouldn't believe that I'd only driven for real once before.

In return for his help I gave him my cash-machine device, skooled him, explained to him a plan of how to use it without running into bandits or getting caught. What to do with the dunzi. Ways to avoid being spotted. Take hotel rooms up in the Smoke for a few nights, steal and launder; avoid an obvious pattern. Split whatever he got with Fi and Dad. It was a shame that I wouldn't get to run this operation myself. A money making machine in his very hands - cushti. Darren's mug was smug as you like. He'd finally made a raise. Nice to make my old treacle happy, I owed him one too.

We drove down Kingsthorpe Grove then up past the Racecourse towards the Abington area; parked up in a back street, walked down to the Welly Road. Darren, hood tight round his face, watched as I showed him how the machine worked. I took a few notes for myself then left him at the roadside with a stack of currency in shoulder bag and the strong desire to accumulate more.

He had juss inspected my first go at hotwiring a car, which I had conducted to his satisfaction.

This time it was a more modest Renault Clio.

I drove alone up to Roger's on the Eastern district.

My own November fire festival had four targets: the school; Roger's tings; the betting shop; and the church where the corpse of the Princess probably really was. They all had to go.

Bonus - I got to create some mayhem, distract the powers that be.

Later as I was fleeing the area I started to think that I should take the events of my rampage, develop them into a funky video game. As I sat on the train out of Buckby, directly under the CCTV cameras, I looked at my reflection. Saw myself in the big black screen of the window blending with the lights outside, and began to work out how the contest would play.

It could have a number of levels that you would have to work through. The overall mission objective would be to guide a character on a storm of cold fury, then to escape. The game would be called: TOTAL SCREWFACE.

It would have a series of phases, or levels that you have to work through. The first leg would be like a cross between a simulation game like SimCity and a strategy game like Age Of Empires. I'd call it, Urban Simian.

You'd have to design and grow an estate, build a community from nothing. You're the gamekeeper. You muss set poverty traps. Snare and abandon your excluded prey, do the needful. Make a jail of geography with invisible locks. You guarantee that hard as your outcast avatars might try, they can't go anywhere, can't leave the reservation behind. Locked out - locked up.

Take the neighbourhood bore it, stress it, sell it poisonous dreams, stigmatise it. Create gangs, set them against each other. Create crime, have everyone at it. Put all the right factors into the mix that would make it turn into the kind of kharzie likely to cause one of its inhabitants to turn severe, burn places to the ground. The characters in this game are not inherently violent, but you muss make a society that is; that shoots sparks of anger at its people – ignites them. Punish the poor in as many ways you can, make as much money as you can from them. Make the system you build addicted to making tings worse.

Deprivation is good, enemies need to be generated. Once you have enough of an underclass, declare hostilities - zero tolerance. Of course the place needs drugs, with laws against them. You can't make an omelette with out introducing some crack. Egg on all those law breaking ceremonies that change a child into fully fledged adult, ready to do bird. Ready to get a tag on their ankle. Get as many young-uns as possible to go into a breeding frenzy; fuck about; muck about; doss about; play up – play up and play the game. Malnourish; mal educate; mal adjust – zone out. You get more points if you can make a significant portion of the frothing population crash off like cheap fizzy-wine corks – regular. You lose if the place functions too well. If none of your people are sent down. If everyone has shelter and a job and hobbies and well functioning supported families and love and friends and sustenance and adequate mental health care and drug'n'alcohol problems sensibly dealt with and low levels of brutality and lots of neighbourliness, in the environmentally friendly endz. If your estate turns out having too much of any of that; nix, null, *nil point*. And you don't get through to level two.

To be successful you have to groom an avatar, manipulate their suffering juss right to be ready for the second level of the game. Make sure at least two-or-three totally shit and traumatic events are endured by any of the avatar characters that it's your job to cultivate during the game. Mash 'em up good and proper. Kill someone they love, have them bullied, give them a drug problem; discharge them from the army fraggled. Make sure that any support they might try and get is inadequate. Happy bunnies don't riot.

It's up to you. Be imaginative. Hurt them deep.

I looked out the window and could see a glow in the west. The train neared where me and Jan used to throw our bottles – as close to my house as the trainline went. The church was already burning. I stopped thinking about my game for a few minutes, took in the distant glow. A glimpse of my handiwork. The train carried on. After a couple of minutes I couldn't see the red in the sky anymore, went back to thinking about level two.

If you're malevolent enough, you reach this next level which is called: Head Fuck. It's like a flight simulator game. You're inside the head of the successful avatar looking out at the world surrounded by thousands of dials, switches and warning lights. You have to operate the character. You have to keep them walking. Feed them. Help them take a shit. Control all the key physical and emotional processes going on inside a human being; eat breakfast; ignore parents; act surly, when not getting own way; doss at school; covet trainers.

You muss strike the avatar with abundant domestic tragedies but particularly you've got to make them feel like they want to have sex constantly, while all the time frustrating their attempts to get some. Fill them up with improbable desire then have them cuss the world off for never living up to the dream of satisfying these excesses, never quell their monstrous pangs. You guide the character through a year of their life until they get to eat a military grade smart-drug that propels them to level three, the thrilling: Amok Run.

The train I had caught from Long Buckby had stopped at Northampton Station. A bunch of tired looking people got into the carriage, a few people got out. I clocked all the faces, no obvious Old Bill. The train pulled off. Leaving Northampton could be so easy. I went back to my work on my game.

If you make it through levels one and two then your successful berserker avatar gets to go on an internationally reported fire wielding rampage fuelled by military drugs. He muss avoid the law, the armed forces, and any have-a-go-heroes. If he's lucky, and you show some skills, he'll burn down all the key targets using the correct improvised weapon systems and will gain maximum points. In this part of the game, you see your hands and your weapons in front of you, your point of view: a first person game like Dad's old favourite, Doom. The first target is the school, weapon of choice IED; plasma and gas. You have to highjack Samantha, take her on a high speed spree.

Joyride, then ditch her.

Then return to the school, to destroy it.

The second target is Roger's flashy wheels, weapon of choice thermite.

You steal a car. Drive across town to the Eastern district. Retrieve the thermite from the hedge outside Roger's and Dot's house; put it on the roof of his car, above the petrol tank. Ignite the shit with a sparkler wand. Then run. More points are awarded for capturing the events on video. This is tricky to do as within three seconds of lighting the stuff with the skinny firework rod, molten metal will pour down through the car melt into the petrol tank; resulting in a gigantic fireball. Roger will then come running out of his house and attempt to chase after you with a baseball bat. A look on his mug that's real fucking magic.

You then escape with the footage, in your discreetly stashed stolen car. Upload the scene to Youtube via your mobile. Points are awarded if you remember to disable the comments section because the only thing you learn from reading those is that most people don't have anything to say and they can't even do that very well.

At the third target you steal a faster car, then hit the turf accountants. Do the bizniz. Weapons of choice vodka Molotov, and improvised flamethrower. Points are deducted if you kill anyone. Points are gained if you scream warnings before letting rip and smile at the CCTV then treat it to the flames. You also gain a banker's bonus if you manage to unzip your cock and piss up against the counter before throwing your flaming Sambuca bomb at the curtains.

Once the place is burning nicely you make your escape and drive. As the darkening sky becomes fully black you reach the upper crusty's church: St Mary the Virgin at Great Brington. There you begin your assault on the fourth and final target. Weapon of choice improvised fuel-air bomb. You use your homemade thermite-putty to burn through the church's locks. Then you muss find your torch inside your bag, this you muss use to navigate the darkened church.

You take the jerrican of petrol which you luckily find in the stolen car. If you don't find it you have to mess about with siphoning and this might jeopardise your mission. You pour fifteen pints of volatile Iraq juice into the tea-urn at the back of the church. One pint for each year since the Princess died - on the night you were born.

The world might have ignored you then, with their mind on other tings. They'll not ignore you now. You leave the rest of the petrol next to the big kettle then you take a digital-plug-timer from your bag, set it to come on in three hundred seconds. Then you stick it in a socket in the wall and plug the tea urn into it. You make sure the power is on so that in five minutes time this giant kettle will start to boil petrol. On the floor, at the opposite end of the building from the fuel, you place a candle that you've found. You light it. A flame flickers casting shadows over the screen that conceals the Princess's final resting place.

To gain some massive 'xtra badman notoriety points to propel yourself into celebrity status and the next level of the game, you muss set up a video camera a bit of distance away from the church. You use the one on your old mobile which you no longer need. You position the phone; wedge it into a nearby tree. You leave it there recording the silent church; lit, so far, juss by external lamps. Then you chip, disappear into the darkness; using the remaining thermite putty to weld the door of the church shut.

The mobile phone footage, familiar from the media frenzy that followed the deed, is the rocking inspiration for the spectacle at the end of level three. You see the church its roof exploding into inferno, a burning beacon on a Northamptonshire hill announcing the last of the first salvos in *my war*.

The Princess's face appears in the fireball that engulfs the ancient building and transforms into Samantha's grief stricken face. You hear a frantic soundtrack of news reports, speculation and sirens.

Sweet and dandy, I was on my way into the future; heading into the darkness. Go deh. I looked out of the train's window, couldn't make out any signs of Northampton. Blud, I'd bolted town; left that world behind, yes.

You've bombed your bridges. No way back now. You have to jump up a level. You're off, running into the fourth and final stage. This is like a three dimensional platform game, similar to Mario, with a maze-like construction. You'd have to play this section by actually going to the locations wearing special glasses that overlay digital information on the world around you. An augmented reality game called, Manic Minor.

You make your way from the church with out being spotted or chased by the various forces that are now after you. Then to Long Buckby, ditch wheels. Catch a train to Wolverton. Follow the canal on foot. Hit country pathways, adjust to the darkness; keep in shadows; walk through streams carrying your backpack; use an OS Map. End up in a forest, right next to the M1, that Vic says the IRA used to use as a weapons dump.

Go to ground.

During this stage of the game you have to jump up through a huge variety of emotional conditions; mental states; levels of awareness that are reflected in the colours, graphics and types of puzzle that have to be solved. The game would monitor your breathing rate; your pulse; your brainwaves; your speed of responses. You have to coach yourself to lower your heart rate by controlling your breathing, while solving increasingly complex puzzles that are overlaid on the world around you by digital goggles that you wear. These brainteasers are everywhere and in everything in this game world. By the time you reach Vic at the end of this level, the conclusion of this edition of the contest, the amount of detail should be full-on; your breath control excellent. The total information in each second of the game so vast only people who have taken the pill will be able to play it to the end.

Each copy of the game ideally would come with a free pill.

We aim to make the drug widely available.

Back at the church juss before I legged it, I wedged my phone between the branches of a tree - onboard camera rolling. I was walking away, when it began to ring. Rushed back to silence it, found it was Fiona. I answered the call. Sudden sadness gummed up my brain, I could hardly think.

I didn't want to leave my sister behind.

"Guess wha?"

I told her to tell me.

"Your spar Darren dashed me a wedge. I'm taking Jan up the cinema – safe yeah?"

I said that was great.

Fiona was perceptive, her mood radar strong, her interrogation technique straightforward.

"So whasup?"

I told her that there was nothing wrong.

She said, "Er, yeah? Who do you think yer chattin' to? Pull da udda brudda."

I told her I wasn't twisting her tit, she started to laugh.

"Come see me."

I sniffled, trying to stop myself from baaling; said I couldn't check her. That she should take a gander at the clip I'd uploaded to the net, that I'd called, Hungry T'ermite Sorcery.

She was near Jan's laptop so set it in motion while she continued to chat-on.

She didn't seem that phased by the commotion with Jan's folks. She was tough in her own way. Roger hadn't beaten that out of her, probably clapped her down for standing up to him. Her feistiness had defo influenced her life, perhaps it ran in the family.

Fiona let out a squeal. I knew she'd seen the footage of Roger's car.

I started to cry. I was happy sad.

Fiona asked me if I was okay, what was wrong. I juss carried on crying. Finally I managed to tell her that I was going away, that I would see her again but that I didn't know when. I wouldn't be dinging her for long time either. Told her to look after Dad, give him some help with his reading. I wanted to let her know that Darren would soon be giving her more moolar. To keep shtumm about it; hide it good; only use a little. But I didn't, in case anyone was listening in. That was frustrating.

She asked me why I had to flee. I wouldn't tell her. She got insistent.

"It's hard sometimes t'say shit...y'don't fink you'll be believed." When she said that, it made me grieve even more.

I fought back my feelings, told her I would tell her; but not now.

I thought about letting her know where to find the phone with its forthcoming footage but changed my mind.

Best if I kept her out of it.

As it was, the Old Bill found the phone anyway.

When I said goodbye I deleted everything from the sim-card; muted all the sounds this time. Then turned the camera back on and put it back into the tree to record the forthcoming show.

Seeing as how I'd had an international hit with my mobile phone footage, perhaps a more straightforward Hollywood production would be the obvious way to tell these events. If I was going to lay this all out cinema style, I'd have to ramp it up even more. Take all the goodness out, fling away the stuff that's in between. Remove the heart. Like some of the class-As. You start by munching the plant then you intensify and intensify. The poppy; opium; heroin: the leaf; cocaine; crack: the truth; the news; films. The truth isn't a popular product. Once the media start to eat you, you might as well floss damax, go whole hog put chops on big screen full-on. Don't know who I'd want to play me, but Idris Elba would be good as Vic.

It's tempting to begin with explosions but I'd start the film where I met Vic, about ten miles from our yard, over in Salcey Forest and then I'd cut back.

EXT. WOODLAND – NIGHT

Police with dogs move through dense trees their hazard jackets catching in torch beams. A helicopter buzzes overhead.

In a clearing a BWOY stumbles gasping for breath. He drops his rucksack then collapses on the ground in exhaustion. In the distance the sounds of a helicopter, the sounds of dogs. He reaches into the bag, removes a human skull, holds it up, looks it in the eye.

BWOY

Well Princess, we gonna make it?

From the bushes, UNCLE VIC silently emerges in full camouflaged combat gear. He stealthily comes up behind the Bwoy, puts his hand over his mouth; breathes into his ear.

                              VIC

                            Shhhh.

The bwoy turns to face Vic.

                             BWOY

                              Vic.

                              VIC

                Good. You didn't recognise me.

INT. KITCHEN – DAD'S PLACE - NIGHT

DAD'S hands pop the lid on a Smartie tube. He inverts
the tube, spilling its multicoloured contents onto a
chaotic kitchen work surface. His fingers rapidly sort
through the sweets separating out the blue ones.

A pill box is shaken. A blue pill falls into Dad's hands.
He places it gently on top of the work surface. He cuts
the pill carefully in half with a Stanley knife. He places
half the pill back into the pill box. He fastens its lid;
pockets it.

The other half of the pill he plants vertically into the
top of the ice cream; concealing the fact that the pill
has been cut. The half-pill stands shining in bright
yellow Cornish ice-cream; its reflection distorted in the

part of the spoon sticking out of the desert. Dad's hands scoop the blue Smarties up. He sprinkles them around the pill onto the afters. He skewers a birthday candle into the top of the ice cream. Takes out a lighter, ignites it; lighting the candle.

He sparks up a half smoked spliff then smiles.

INT. LIVING ROOM – DAD'S PLACE – NIGHT

Dad, holding the ice cream, walks into the main room where the Bwoy is energetically playing a video game. There is one birthday card sitting on top of the TV. Dad shoves the ice cream under his nose. Bwoy momentarily looks annoyed at the interruption; then grins.

DAD

Fussborn!

BWOY

Yush!

DAD

'Appy birthday picney.

It didn't all go down like this but you've got to pepper things, get gritty, to pull in the punters. Even though he's shown spiking me, the scene with Dad is probably a bit too mellow for the big screen. I should have Dad grab me then stick a hypo in my throat. Filled with a bright blue fluid he injects it straight into my jugular, leaves me spasming on the floor baaling out electric whale song.

It doesn't matter that I never captured the Princess's skull, that wasn't really at the forefront anymore. I did recognise Vic too. It was only later that Vic was to perform plastic surgery on his own face, which come to think of it might make a better opening scene.

The stuff I made up about Dad was probably pretty accurate. He had cut the pill in half. He passed it to me on the ice-cream like I described.

First thing I knew about it being cut in half was when he handed me the remaining bit, when I told him that I was going to meet with Vic. Too chicken to take it himself, he obviously didn't want to end up like me. I was tempted to give it to Fiona, but I didn't get a chance.

The Police didn't follow. There were no dogs. As I picked my way across the cold country to Hartwell, in the extreme distance juss one helicopter. I saw it hover in the sky moving slowly towards me. Heard its manic bass pulse as its blades sliced the air. For a moment I thought they'd sniffed out my trail. I thought of ways to try and reduce my infra-red signal.

You can see a long way from up there. I'd eyeballed for myself how far when Sam arranged for me to go up in an Apache. That seemed like time ago, but it was only a few weeks. Sitting raised behind the pilot, I got a good all-round survey of the cockpit. It felt like my head was dangerously close to the rotors. The whole machine looks bad, predatory, intimidating; alien. It's noisy inside, disorientating. The guy flying looked half-cyborg. His black visor made him look like an insectobot. Kind of how I want the people who play the final stage of my game to look, this was augmented reality - original. Details from the targeting systems integrated into the helmet and display sight system.

From where that chopper was an Apache could take me out, but a police helicopter probably had no chance of seeing me miles away in the dark. It suddenly changed direction and moved away rapidly. Wonder if it even was the filth on board, it was more likely some bizniz tycoon flying out of Silverstone. At least for now the police had no call for thirty millimetre guns, laser guided Hellfire missiles and a Longbow radar system like the Apache had on board. At twenty three million quid a pop, probably a bit out of their price range.

There was no obvious threat. The helicopter moved almost out of sight, following the motorway back towards town. I doubted that they had anything on their consoles that would pick me up. Likely to have seen my handy work from up there though, burning merrily to the North of them. Maybe it was the international press flying in.

I wondered if my dream power was strong enough to develop other new skills after a brief exposure, or if my driving game playing had somehow been transferred from one part of my brain to another during sleep. Perhaps I could fly an Apache? I'd been in one. I'd played simulation games. I thought perhaps if I could engineer getting into one again I might find out. That could be jokes.

But first I'd have to sleep on it, see what happened. When I finally got to the forest I was knackered. I could have slept right there but I didn't. I kept vigilant. I sat in damp woodland on my own till Vic showed up.

The idea of digging up the Princess, of fame, was got me the ASBO but my actions didn't get me a high level of notoriety. Funny, once I stopped wanting it, it came for me like an octopus; ink and tentacles and darkness.

Attention probably wasn't so clever a thing to attract. This time I wanted to disappear. Capture was not on the menu. Draw a line under my previous life, leave Samantha behind. Got a bit carried away in the spectacle creation department.

Accidentally I tied myself into that popular media storyline, psycho kids who kick off western worldwide shoot up schools and shopping centres; promoters of pure celebrity, killing for vanity on CCTV. Others blow themselves up for seemingly deeper reasons. But they get to have their poster on the holy wall, bleat out their martyrdom videos into cyberspace. Twenty First century love. Getting what they can't get elsewhere. Aiming for the mother of all crimes; none will be remembered for very long but probably longer than constructive deeds. Stop someone on the street ask them the name of the Prime Minster, or a hit song, from a hundred years ago. A good chance they won't know. Ask them the name of a sex case slayer from back then and they'll probably say Jack the Ripper. It's clear that being maximum cold and dark has fame longevity and if you're original too, it burns long in our national mind.

Murder is too easy.

I wasn't going to sink to that level; dash out death. I had other plans.

Celebrity is boring, there's no reason to look up to it, to listen to my yap juss because of it. It's not what others imagine of you that's important but what you think of yourself. You muss hold your corner.

It doesn't really matter if you're remembered because it won't be for very long anyway. In the end it'll all be baking dust. Sooner rather than later if we don't pull our fingers out of our arses.

Keep it real.

The school, Sam and nex' man, they had had their chance to help me; now I would help myself.

The truth, once seen never forgiven. How much were they spending on this operation? How many dollars did they fling down? They could have put some of that effort into genuinely trying to help me. Juss like when they wasted the tens of thousands putting my Dad in a prison and he can still barely read.

My justified flames only destroyed a few buildings but they heralded my growing plans to ignite a widespread rebellion, which I intended to ferment in time with the help of more of those blue pills.

Bredrin, laters.

During my research at the school I read about Isaac Newton, when he was a kid he'd threatened to burn his mother alive in her house and he went on to make a major contribution to science, to the world of knowledge. No one knows how they're going to develop. Even in the deepest shadow there is some light. Norman was right, all life is precious. Priceless art worthless compared to it; even though our economy is rigged up with the reverse in mind. The gun that shot Dex - one of Dad's prison spars - blew off the side of his head in a back street in Bricky, was made by a British firm and sold for Balkan wars. When the tide of hostilities turned the weapon floated back to English shores, a salmon of death returning home to spawn. What electric blow-back might I taste from the device I'd sold Duggy?

One day I would return home too, but not to kill.

There were other ways to fight.

With Vic's help I would become a new kind of soldier.

END

Also Available from Lepus Books:

"Book Thirteen"
A novel by A. William James (aka Jamie Delano)

"Leepus | DIZZY"
A novel by Jamie Delano

"The Things You Do"
A memoir by Deborah Delano

"The Saddest Sound"
A novel by Deborah Delano

"Wilful Misunderstandings"
A collection of short stories by Richard Foreman

And coming in 2016:

"Leepus | THE RIVER"
A second 'Leepus' novel by Jamie Delano

Lightning Source UK Ltd.
Milton Keynes UK
UKOW02f1250190516

274580UK00002B/78/P